DIRTY DORMS AND FRESH MEN

PETER SCHUTES   CHUCK IDGAF   J. W. STEED

Four hot stories carry a heavy course load. Add a class, drop your pants, show your ass, and have a gas!

UNDER THE BOARDWALK - UC Santa Cruz student Harry Shore needs money for books and supplies. He takes a job at the boardwalk, where he meets a security guard with an enormous capacity to fulfill Harry's desires.

DORMITORY URGES - A junior in college has a sexual awakening when he realizes that he likes men with big furry bellies. When he meets a big bear of a student named Ryan, he gets to fulfill his fantasy.

SLEAZY A - Our narrator has a tremendous knack for getting what he wants in the campus bathrooms. He submits to the professors, but then he meets a handsome student who teaches him how to be more active in bed.

THE TEAROOM IN THE TREES - A language student of epic proportions frequents the campus tearoom for occasional relief. A chance encounter with a big bodybuilder sends him into the wild. If the trees could talk!

CONTENTS

UNDER THE BOARDWALK

by Peter Schutes

AMUSEMENT PARK

Since he was old enough to stand, Harry Shore's favorite place on Earth was the Santa Cruz Boardwalk. Every summer, he and his parents stayed at a motel near the beach called the Sandpiper Inn. He heard the sound of the rollercoaster roaring long past his bedtime. The room was lit by the flashing lights and neon glow of the amusement park. Despite many troubles and unhappy times, the weekend at the beach was always a sanctuary for Harry. It was something he could rely on for most of his childhood.

When Harry applied to UC Berkeley, he was deferred to UC Santa Cruz. His mother and father didn't have a lot of extra money, so he was going to have to work. Like a fool, he chose to work on the boardwalk, thinking it would be the most fun anyone could have. He found out quickly that visiting an amusement park is very different from working there. His eyes were opened to the terrible people of the world who lived to make minimum-wage employees suffer. It was a rude awakening.

Even though he was nearly a man, Harry still had the skin of a child. Despite his name, he was hairless and smooth. He looked in envy at the boys around him whose chest hair had sprouted. He also had determined that he was less than gifted in between his legs. His hairless pubic mound was topped by a thumb-sized penis that hardened but never really grew.

Working at the boardwalk, you had to leave your uniform in your designated locker each night. This meant changing out of his civilian jeans and t-shirt at the start of the shift and changing back at the end. Harry wore boxer shorts to keep the mystery of his tiny penis from being revealed.

Many of the guys liked to shower before the shift. Harry wished he had the courage to join them, but he was too ashamed of his hairless body and tiny penis. To make matters worse, ever since puberty, he had stopped thinking about girls, and all his fantasies were centered around hairy men.

Lost in one such fantasy, he was startled out of his reverie by a colossal hunk of a security guard.

"Oh, sorry bro. My locker's right next to yours. Do you mind?"

Harry shook his head and looked at the floor. The security guard stuck out a hand.

"Name's Cleve."

"Harry."

Cleve guffawed. "Not really living up to your name, eh?" Cleve thwacked a meaty paw on Harry's chest.

Harry looked up at his tormentor. The security guard wore thick horn-rimmed glasses. His hair was cut military style. His jaw was square, and his arms were like long, furry balloons with bulging biceps. A thick thatch of chest hair sprouted out of the collar of his t-shirt. Harry swallowed.

Cleve stammered. "I mean, sorry man if that was out of line."

Harry smiled. "It's no problem. I'm probably too sensitive about it."

Cleve grinned. "You hitting the showers?" As he asked, he stripped off his jeans and t-shirt, revealing his gloriously furry muscular form. Cleve hitched his thumbs in the waistband of his jockey shorts and peeled them off, revealing a powerful set of glutes and a monster-sized dick.

Harry said, "S-sure. Yeah." He let his boxers drop, waiting for more humiliation.

Instead, Cleve leaned in. "God damn, I like the little ones." With that, he threw a towel over his shoulder and strutted to the showers, his massive dong swinging from thigh to thigh. Harry wrapped his towel around his waist and scampered after him.

They were the only two in the showers. Cleve waited for Harry to pick a shower head, then took the one right next to him.

"Do you like to fuck?" Cleve didn't pull any punches.

Harry blushed. "I think so, yeah."

Cleve said, "Oh my god, are you a virgin?"

Harry turned a darker shade of crimson.

"No, no, don't sweat it, dude. I'm an expert. Breaking in virgins is my favorite."

Harry was done being ashamed. "With that big thing?"

Cleve wasn't bothered. "Yeah. I'm like the John Bonham of ass fucking. It's a gift."

Harry was hard as a rock. Cleve reached across and rubbed Harry's glorified clit. "Oh, I'll bet you come like a sprinkler."

It was true. Harry's bedroom walls at home required regular cleaning. His dorm room was a double, so he rarely got a chance to get off.

Cleve asked, "Do you live nearby?"

Harry shook his head. "I'm up at the college."

Cleve said, "A banana slug. Nice. I live in Aptos. With my folks."

Harry looked at the bodybuilder who had to be almost thirty. "Do you like living at home?"

Cleve laughed. "Hell no! But this shit job doesn't pay enough for an apartment. I'm saving up."

Harry looked between Cleve's legs. The man's cock was nearly double the size and standing at a 45-degree angle. It was too heavy to stand tall.

A few more people came in. Harry turned away, but Cleve just stood there, grinning, while the other guys checked out his semi. Nobody in there could hold a candle to Cleve.

"Come on, Harry, our shift doesn't start for another twenty minutes. Let me show you something."

Wrapped in his towel Cleve led Harry to a stairwell going into the dark.

"What is this place?"

Cleve smiled. "Under the Boardwalk."

The dark cave at the bottom of the stairs smelled of body fluids and ass sweat. Cleve held up a bottle of baby oil.

"I keep this down here for just such an emergency." He knelt, putting his mustache on Harry's virgin ass. His tongue darted in and out of the tight pink hole. Harry couldn't believe how good it felt.

"Oh, shit."

Cleve didn't say anything; he just kept slobbering and kissing the hole until it was slippery. They lay flat in a sixty-nine, Cleve underneath Harry, licking his asshole. Harry took the first couple of inches of Cleve's thick cock in his mouth. When Cleve pushed deeper, Harry coughed. The slick saliva coated Cleve's cock, making it slippery. It was easier and easier for Cleve to push his way past Harry's tonsils. And each time Harry gagged, the cock got more and more slippery.

Cleve coated Harry's ass in baby oil and used the rest to lubricate his cock. With his powerful arms, he came to a sitting position and held Harry dangling just above his cock. Harry steadied himself by holding on to Cleve's massive shoulders.

In a gentle motion, Cleve lowered Harry down onto the throbbing head of his cock. Harry felt the tip go in. It didn't hurt even a little, so he breathed a sigh of relief. Then Harry lowered him another inch. Suddenly, Harry's ass was on fire. But just as quickly, Cleve lifted him off.

"It gets better, I promise." He thrust upward, forcing his head past the sphincter. There was a loud pop as Harry's shitter closed around the thin space below the corona.

Cleve held the boy. "Are you good?"

Harry nodded. "Is it in?"

Cleve said, "A little bit." At the same time, he lowered Harry downward, stopping only when the fat head hit the bottom of Harry's rectum.

"Ooooowwww!" Harry tried to stand up, but Cleve's powerful arms held him in place.

"Just count backward from ten. Out loud. Let me hear you."

Harry struggled, but he started counting. By the time he reached four, it didn't hurt. In fact, it felt good.

Cleve said, "Okay, just one more thing." He tilted Harry to the left and thrust upwards. With another loud pop, Cleve forced his way into Harry's sigmoid colon.

Harry cried, but the pain subsided quickly. He was filled with Cleve's giant cock.

In a movement out of Olympic wrestling, Cleve whirled Harry around so he was on all fours doggy style. Then the fucking started.

Cleve's fat cock pressed up against the prostate gland. Harry's little penis drooled sticky precum all over the filthy, sandy floor under the boardwalk. Cleve cupped his hand like he was drinking from a mountain stream.

"Sweet boy cum. Makes me fucking horny!" He picked up the pace of the fucking, holding Harry around the hips to keep him from flying forward.

Harry had attained nirvana. He groaned softly, taking tiny gulps of air to keep from passing out from the pleasure. Each time Cleve pounded in, Harry felt filled to the totality of his being. On each outstroke, it was a sense of relief like when taking a massive shit. The strokes grew longer and longer until pretty soon the bodybuilder could pull all the way out before plunging easily back in through the loose hole that had once been Harry's anus. In those moments, Harry felt cool ocean air blowing through the gap.

"You won't hear your farts for a month, but it'll be worth it."

Something about the cockiness with which Cleve said it made Harry shoot a load. He shot his wad on the ground so hard, it splattered onto Cleve's balls and knees.

"Oh, fuck yeah, kid. That's so fucking hot." Harry felt Cleve fondle his little bits, before slurping the juice from his hand. The action was so depraved and sexy, it made Harry hard again.

Cleve slapped his ass once, twice, three times. "You like it, don't you Harry?"

Harry was well beyond the use of words, so he just moaned appreciatively.

"Yeah. I'm gonna fuck your little ass again and again. You won't walk right."

Again, the dirty talk made Harry come. Again, Cleve slurped it up in his hand.

"You come like a bitch. I'm giving you multiple orgasms, right?"

Harry nodded. Cleve started to take smaller strokes.

"Oh fuck, man, I'm close."

"Come inside me." Harry wanted the man's cum deep inside his guts.

Cleve said, "Okay, hang on." He grabbed Harry's hair and pulled his head back. "You like that?"

"Yes, sir."

Cleve let go of the hair and grabbed the boy by the hands, pulling him close so he could fuck with abandon. The popping sound grew louder as Cleve's fat head poked past the rectum over and over, harder and harder.

"Oh shit, Harry. I'm gonna fucking come. I'm gonna fucking come. I'm gonna..."

Harry felt a warm tide flowing deep inside him. Cleve made animal grunts. He let go of the boy's arms, and collapsed on top of him, gyrating his hips to plant his seed as deep as possible. Harry felt Cleve's hot breath on his neck. They stayed joined dick to ass for a few minutes until Harry couldn't keep him inside any longer. In a long, slithering motion, Cleve's soft cock snaked its way out of his insides, landing on the floor with a loud thwack. A small waterfall of cum gushed out of the gaping hole. Cleve licked the sticky hole until it snapped shut.

Harry turned to look at the man who took his virginity. He traced circles around the hairy nipples. Cleve took one hand and put it on his square jaw. They kissed. Harry tasted cum on Cleve's breath.

Harry asked, "What's next?"

Cleve laughed. "Show up early tomorrow, and you'll find out."

2

BUNCH OF BALLOONS

Cleve hadn't lied. The next day, Harry walked with a slight limp. When he released some pent-up gas, it came out as barely a whisper. Changing into his uniform, he winced a little when he lifted a leg. The uniform was comprised of brown polyester pants and a 50/50 old-timey barbershop quartet button-up shirt with an arm garter and a straw hat. Harry thought he should get hardship pay for having to dress like his great-grandfather.

Harry liked working the juice cart because there were long stretches with nothing to do. Unlike corn dogs or popcorn, the juice was not very popular. It was sugar, artificial flavor, dye, and water in a container designed to look like the fruit it was meant to portray. So purple sugar water came in a grape-shaped container. Orange water came in a plastic orange. Fruit punch, inexplicably, came in a red globe that must be the "fruit" from which fruit punch was derived.

All this free time between juice sales meant he could surreptitiously read a book. Management frowned on such activity, but they weren't exactly breathing down his neck.

Harry didn't see Cleve in the locker room. He felt a puppy-like attraction to the swaggering security guard who took his virginity. He hung his head and headed out onto the boardwalk with his cart full of meaning-less juice.

There was a balloon vendor who made Harry's heartstrings zing. He was close to Harry's age, blond, green eyes, definitely a surfer in the off hours. His name tag simply said "George". That afternoon, George walked past Harry's juice cart at least a half dozen times. Balloon vendors wore knickers and newsboy hats. George filled out the front and back of his knickers quite nicely. His butt was encased in poly-ester. His soft cock was visible down one leg. It was tight enough that you could tell he was circumcised.

When Harry took his dinner break, the cafeteria was packed. He spied an empty spot at a table and asked if it was taken. George said, "Nope, buddy, have a seat."

Harry reddened and sat down, hoping George hadn't noticed.

"Harry, right?"

"Yeah, how did you know?"

George snorted. "Your name tag, dumbass!" It wasn't mean. It was playful.

"Oh, right." Harry balanced a piece of wilted ice-berg lettuce on his spork before eating it.

George pointed to the crappy salad. "The entire US supply of iceberg lettuce grows right near here. But it goes down to LA before it comes back up here. By the time they serve it to us, it's brown. Ironic, right?"

Harry smiled. "Yeah, pretty ironic."

George asked, "Do you study at UCSC?"

Harry nodded.

"Me too. I'm a Philosophy major. And you?"

"History. I'm going into Law, hopefully."

George grabbed Harry's arm. "A lawyer? I'm gonna need a sugar daddy with my major. Shall I give you my number?"

Harry was shocked that George was even remotely into him. He decided to play along.

"Yes. I've been looking for someone to spoil."

George snorted again. His laugh was both annoying and endearing in equal measure.

Then George whispered in Harry's ear. "I'll earn my keep. I'll fuck you silly."

Harry felt his little penis stiffen. Why was this blond god into him? He knew he would blow his chances if he didn't respond. He leaned in and whispered in George's ear. "I'll take a free sample right now."

George grinned. "Under the Boardwalk."

The two young men scampered down the stairwell, only to find Cleve down there fucking a newbie.

"Over there." The security guard held up a finger pointing deeper into the inky darkness of this bizarre subterranean fuck den.

George took Harry's hand and walked him into the dark. Harry felt George's hands undo his pants and slide them down. He heard a zipper and felt a huge stiff cock brush his bare bottom. He heard George spit repeatedly, then George's wet finger went into Harry's hole.

George said, "Damn dude, you're loose."

Cleve hollered from afar. "You're welcome!"

Harry was glad it was too dark for anyone to see him blush.

George worked two, then three fingers into Harry's ass.

"Are you ready?"

"Yeah. Put it in."

George spat a couple more times, stroked his cock, then pushed his way in. George wasn't as thick as Cleve, and he was about the same length. When George hit the back wall, he maneuvered and easily slid past into the colon. Harry shivered. It felt so good. George's style wasn't as brutal as Cleve's. His strokes were fast but gentle.

"Oh, your ass is so smooth, Harry. It's perfect."

Harry reached back and rubbed George's ass. He could feel the powerful glutes contract with each forward thrust. It was softer than Cleve's.

From across the room, Harry heard Cleve shout "Oh fuck yeah! Fuck! Oh, fuck! I'm coming."

The little guy he was fucking said, "Yeah, do it. Come in me."

Their non-verbal cries of lust echoed off the discarded furniture. And then the little guy ran up the stairs.

George was in a groove, fucking Harry. They were both startled when Cleve wandered over.

"Make room. I want some of that."

George said, "Dude, what the fuck?"

Cleve said, "Watch and learn."

Cleve pushed Harry lower, then raised his leg and hopped onto Harry's back. With great effort, he forced his cock beside George's and forced his way in.

Harry let out a shriek. Cleve's dick on its own had nearly split him in two. With George's already inside, it burned. George stopped complaining and let Cleve's huge hog slide back and forth along his.

"Shit, dude, that's fucking hot."

Harry had been spoiled by Cleve's fat hog. George felt good, but he wasn't thick enough to satisfy Harry.

With Cleve's added bulk, Harry was more satisfied than he could have dreamed. The pain subsided and was replaced with a throbbing lust. Two big dicks slipping and sliding inside him was enough to send Harry panting and moaning.

George's breath quickened pace. "Dude, I'm close."

Harry nodded, even though no one could see him. He was speechless from pleasure. Suddenly, the pleasure spread in rapid waves, causing his insides to pulse.

Cleve grunted. "You're coming like a girl, Harry."

It was true. Harry felt orgasmic ripples all up and down his insides. The contractions milked the two cocks.

George said, "I can't hold it. What are you doing? Fuck!" Harry felt a hot flood of young-man cum. It caused his contractions to increase.

Cleve pounded hard and rough. "Shit, that's fucking hot."

The muscular man sawed back and forth in sync with the contractions. When he reached down to touch Harry's little hard cock, it was too much. Harry came all over Cleve's hand.

"Oh fuck, that's too hot. I'm coming."

Cleve leaned back, sucking the air. For a second time, Harry was filled to overflowing with a warm river. George stayed deep inside Harry, keeping George's soft cock trapped. At last, Cleve's fat dick shrank and softened. Harry involuntarily expelled the two soft cocks, leaving a huge puddle on the cement floor.

George had a radium watch. "Shit! I got like three minutes to get back out there."

He buttoned up and ran.

Cleve pinched Harry's smooth nipple very hard. "Fucking around on me already?"

Harry was stunned. "Uh, I could say the same for you."

Cleve guffawed. "I'm just messing with you. An ass as sweet as yours belongs to everyone."

3

HOT BUTTERED POPCORN

The next night, just as the boardwalk closed and Harry's shift was about to end, Mike, his manager, came and asked for help. Mike was pretty shaken. There had been an injury when the popcorn cart exploded. It was a long walk down the nearly abandoned boardwalk to the alcove where the popcorn cart was stationed. A layer of butter-flavored grease coated the cart's interior.

"Is he okay?"

Mike nodded. "He got some burns. The first aid station said he was going to be alright. Just first-degree. But shit, nobody should have to go through that."

The manager's walkie-talkie exploded to life with another emergency in the arcade.

"Will you be okay here? I'll send someone to help."

Harry shrugged. "Yeah. I hate cleaning."

Mike handed him gloves, a tall shaker of Boraxo, and a putty knife. "Just sprinkle, scrape and toss. Don't use water yet. Help is on its way."

Mike scurried off, leaving Harry to degrease the tiny kitchen and cash register. Harry started on the ceiling. He powdered the grease and scraped it, letting the shavings fall to the greasy floor. Harry put one foot in the cart to reach further. When he put his weight on it, it went out from under him. He did the splits, one leg on the ground and the other stretched to the far wall of the cart. He was stuck. He couldn't get enough purchase on the greasy floor to push off.

"Mmm. That's some buttery popcorn."

Harry knew that voice anywhere. He felt two big hands cup his taut ass.

"Help, Cleve, I'm stuck."

"I know. It's kinda hot." Cleve's big paw reached down the back of Harry's ass and tickled his hole. Harry squirmed. He was annoyed and excited in equal measure. Cleve's free hand cupped Harry's crotch.

"You little devil. Is that a golf pencil in your pocket, or are you just happy to see me?"

Harry was trapped, hard, humiliated, and hungry for dick.

"Cleve, my manager is sending someone to help. You gotta stop."

Cleve snickered. "Who do you think he sent?"

Harry realized just how trapped he was. It was deeply arousing.

Cleve said, "Oops." There was a loud ripping sound. "Gee dude, when you did the splits you tore your pants." Another ripping sound. "There, now it's big enough."

Cleve scraped butter grease off the counter and stuck it through Harry's pants. One finger slipped in smoothly, then two. Harry squirmed and wriggled. He liked being so powerless with such a powerful hunk of a man.

When the third finger made its way in, Cleve's hot breath tickled Harry's neck.

"You ready for it, boy?"

"Yes."

Cleve said, "Yes, what?"

"Yes, sir. Fuck me, sir."

Harry could hear a buckle being unfastened, a zipper coming down, and flesh against polyester as Cleve struggled to free himself from his uniform.

"Damn, boy, I'm trapped too. Hang on." The three fingers left Harry's hole. He looked over his shoulders and could see Cleve greasing up his long fat cock.

"Turn around and wait for it, bitch." Cleve was really into the dominator role. Harry liked being submissive.

Harry felt the tickle of a mustache on his butt cheeks, then Cleve's forceful tongue invaded his hole. He slurped and slobbered like a dog eating peanut butter.

"You taste good with butter." They both laughed.

Clutching his foot-long cock, Cleve put one foot on the step and pressed forward. Harry's eyes fluttered as he gasped. Cleve's cock always felt like the first time. There was blinding pain, but it slowly dissolved into pleasure as Cleve pushed farther. He rounded the corner and pushed home. Harry felt Cleve's strong hips slam into his buttocks.

"Fuck me."

Cleve smacked Harry's face hard. "Fuck me, what?"

"Fuck me, sir."

Harry felt the thick log withdraw almost to the tip, then slide and snake its way into his guts. Then again, and a third time, and a fourth, until Harry lost count. Cleve shortened the strokes and quickened his pace. Harry went to that place that felt so good, it should only be reserved for the afterlife. Every nerve in his body was singing.

Cleve smacked his ass. "Tighten that hole"

Harry obeyed. He gripped the monstrous pole with his ass muscles and squeezed.

"Oh fuck, yeah. Just like that."

Harry squeezed over and over, like a bodybuilder doing reps.

"Dude slow down. You're gonna make me come."

Harry wriggled and squeezed, doing everything he could to give Cleve a fraction of the satisfaction he was getting from him.

"I'm serious. Oh shit. Oh shit. Fuck. I'm gonna come."

"Come inside me."

Cleve reached around and massaged Harry's little nub through the cloth of his pants. Harry didn't think it was possible to be more satisfied by a man, but Cleve proved him wrong.

"You want my load?"

"Yes, sir."

"Good boy." Cleve turned up the pace on his fucking so fast that Harry lost his grip. His ass just let go and accepted that enormous cock completely. The sound of Cleve's cock pounding into him made loud clapping noises. The clapping grew louder and faster until soon it was a standing ovation at the Symphony.

"Oh shit! Oh shit!" Cleve tipped over the edge. Holding and squeezing Harry's penis, he pulled the boy tight, so the entire length of his cock was inside.

A hot flooding sensation alerted Harry that Cleve was cumming.

"Yeah. Yeah. Oh damn, Harry, you're so fucking fine."

As he came down off the high of Cleve's pounding, Harry realized his crotch was soaking wet. He had shot his load in his underwear and didn't even realize it. The orgasm in his guts was so much more intense that Harry wanted to feel it forever. His penis was small. His cavernous ass was a much bigger surface. It was still throbbing with Cleve buried deep inside.

Cleve took one step back. His cock came halfway out. He took a second step, and it fell, hitting his leg hard. Behind it, a stream of popcorn butter and cum ran down Harry's leg, staining the pants.

"Are you gonna help me out?"

"What's the magic word?"

Harry rolled his eyes. "Will you help me out of here, sir?"

Cleve gripped Harry's waist and lifted him like he was picking up an empty laundry basket. He planted Harry on the ground.

From behind them came a voice.

"What the fuck is going on here?" It was Mike. He stood with his hands on his hips. "I told you to help him, Cleve, not fuck him!"

4

SUGAR SHACK

Cleve's grin betrayed a little fear. "You're not gonna write me up again, are you?"

Mike's finger danced in the air like he was adding up the pros and cons on an invisible abacus. "Alright, tell you what." He unbuttoned the top button of his black polyester manager pants. "We can work something out."

Mike led them through the empty park and backstage to a shack under the rollercoaster that was always locked. He produced a key. He held the door shut.

"You two gotta promise me you're not gonna say anything."

They nodded. "Well alright then." The tiny shack had little more than a couch, an old black and white TV, and a water cooler. A tub of Vaseline sat atop the television.

Cleve whispered in Harry's ear. "Wait till you see it."

Mike took off his pants. His white legs were covered in thick black fur. His dick was rock hard. It wasn't very long, but much thicker than Cleve's. Mike took off his bow tie and pulled off his button-down shirt. The thick fur covered his chest, neck, shoulders, and back, then ran down the crack of his ass. He looked like a gorilla with a half-log of liverwurst between his legs. The maintenance crews were doing ghost runs on the coaster. It roared over the shack, shaking everything.

Mike rubbed his hands together like a Disney villain. "Harry, I've wanted your fine ass since the day you applied to work here."

Cleve stepped forward. "Hold up, Mike. He's just a kid. You can fuck me. His ass is mine."

Harry was touched and annoyed. He thought it brave of Cleve to protect him, but he was intrigued by the impossibly huge chunk of meat jutting straight toward him.

Mike said, "You're just afraid he'll be stretched so wide you won't feel anything when you fuck him."

Harry put a hand on Cleve's shoulder. "It's okay. I can handle it." He wasn't sure he could, but his curiosity was stronger than his fear.

Mike said, "Don't worry. Neither of you is leaving here until I've crashed both your gates wide open. Harry, you're first."

Mike took a glob of Vaseline and rubbed it on his fat cock while Harry undressed. He took what was left and used it to fit two fingers into Harry's hole, making it slippery.

"Nice. Such a pretty asshole. Not for long."

Mike pushed his greasy dick head against Harry's hole. It didn't move. Mike pushed harder, and the tip found its way in. Another push and Harry saw stars.

"Ow! Fuck!"

Mike pulled back. "Trust me, Harry."

Cleve watched the struggle. "Mike, if the kid can't take it, don't force it."

Harry said, "I can take it!" He hated being underestimated.

"Good." Mike pushed hard, forcing the whole head in. He stopped there and waited.

Harry pounded the ugly sofa. "Fuck! Fuck! Take it out!"

Mike shook his head. "The worst part is over. Just wait."

Sure enough, the horrible tearing, burning pain subsided after a minute.

Cleve couldn't hide his hard-on. Seeing Mike's monster work its way into Harry's ass was a huge turn-on.

Mike said, "Harry, help Cleve out. Suck him off."

Cleve pulled down his polyester pants. The waistband was nearly to his knees before the long, thick meat sprang free from the fabric. It was so long, Harry didn't have to move much to get the head in his mouth. It was too thick for his mouth, but he wanted to please Cleve, so he stretched his jaws apart and let the whole head in.

While Harry swallowed Cleve's cock, Mike held the boy's hips and ground his way deeper. With a series of short back-and-forth thrusts, he forced himself all the way inside. The blunt cock hit the end of Harry's rectum and pressed. It wasn't long enough to turn the corner.

Harry opened wide as if to scream. Cleve took it as a sign he wanted more, and he blocked the airway with his meat, so no scream escaped. Now Harry was impaled at both ends like a pig at a barbecue. Another ghost coaster rocked the hut.

Mike was fairly brutal with his fucking. He hit the

back wall of Harry's hole so many times, it started to pound on his bladder. Before he knew it, Harry was pissing on the floor.

"I'm fucking the piss out of you. I love it!"

Harry was embarrassed but couldn't say anything with his mouth full. Cleve pressed past Harry's tonsils, giving him a clear shot down the boy's throat. The throat muscles gave way, letting the whole length of Cleve's cock press against the voice box. Harry's throat swelled like a boa constrictor swallowing a cat. Cleve pulled back, allowing Harry to retch and catch his breath.

Mike's furry body was covered in sweat. Little droplets dangled from his eyebrows and mustache, falling on Harry's smooth backside. Mike's furry legs and belly rubbed against his skin, tickling him.

"You like that, boy?"

Harry nodded. It was nothing like being fucked by Cleve, but it was enjoyable. He hated how he kept pissing himself, but being filled beyond capacity was exhilarating. The pleasure was doubled with Cleve's magnificent cock fucking his throat.

It was a surprise when Cleve suddenly flooded his throat with cum.

Cleve said, "I'm sorry. I should have said something. I just never had a good blow job before."

Harry swallowed as Cleve pulled out of his mouth. "It was good?"

Cleve laughed. "You took the whole fuckin' thing! Nobody does that."

Harry rubbed his throat tenderly. Cleve's thick cock had nearly torn his esophagus.

Mike said, "I only got one load in me and I want to fuck you, Cleve. It's your turn."

Cleve groaned. "Fine, fuck me."

Harry watched as Mike put his battering ram of a cock against Cleve's tight hole. Cleve's muscles bulged as he bent over and prepared for battle. Harry got hard watching Cleve struggle to take Mike's fat meat. The muscle man's eyes rolled back in his head. Mike wasn't as gentle with him as had been with Harry. He didn't wait, just forced his way fully forward and back.

"Fuck! You fucking bastard!"

Mike laughed. "You've taken it before."

This surprised Harry. It even made him jealous. But seeing Cleve so vulnerable made Harry even harder.

Mike sawed back and forth. Cleve's muscles relaxed as he grew accustomed to the battering ram in his butt.

Cleve caught Harry's eye. "Come here."

Harry stepped forward. Cleve put a meaty paw on Harry's ass and pulled him to his mouth. He sucked on Harry's tiny penis and licked his balls. It was all too much for Harry. He came in Cleve's mouth so hard, it overflowed. Cleve swallowed as much of the sweet juice as he could.

Mike's painfully thick cock had caused Cleve to soften, but swallowing Harry's cum made him rock hard. Harry didn't want to see it go to waste. He got on all fours underneath Cleve. Cleve guided his cock into Harry's hole. Harry did a modified yoga pose to push the cock further inside him. Cleve took tiny thrusts. Mike had certainly loosened him, but it was still a tight fit for Cleve's hefty cock.

Harry got hard again. Something about Cleve's muscular sweat turned him on. The musky aroma was sexier than Mike's. Cleve was all the way in, deep in the sigmoid colon. It made Harry dribble.

Mike pulled out of Cleve. "Fuck. I can never come. I gotta jack off."

He sat on the couch, encircling his cock with both hands, tugging up and down. He watched Cleve masterfully fuck Harry.

Cleve picked up Harry and spun him around to face him. Harry wrapped his legs around Cleve's hips and his arms around his neck. Cleve lifted him up and down, bouncing him like he was playing "Ride-a-Horse".

Harry moaned. He put a nipple in his mouth, chewing gently.

"Oh fuck, Harry. Oh, man." Cleve wriggled in ecstasy. "Suck my titties."

Harry alternated nipples, nursing like a hungry baby. His thigh was wet. His little penis had caused a little river to run down his leg. Cleve was milking him from the inside.

Mike saw the wet spot. He jerked himself faster. "Oh shit, Cleve, he's squirting like a girl."

Cleve didn't hear Mike. He was too far gone in ecstasy. He was buried to the hilt inside the hairless boy who was pushing him closer and closer to orgasm with his nipple sucking.

Just as another roller coaster roared overhead, Harry was overcome. His whole body vibrated. His insides clutched Cleve's cock and twisted it. He couldn't stop the contractions. He was having an orgasm on the inside.

Cleve slapped Harry's ass. "Fuck, boy, you're squeezing me hard! Oh, fuck that's so good."

The slap put Harry over the bump. His little penis sprayed a shower of cum all over the room.

Mike saw the hands-free orgasm. It sent him over. His ridiculously fat cock gushed from the top. The cum didn't shoot upwards, it just gushed out of the tip and rolled down the head like a summer ice cream cone. His hands were covered with cum.

Cleve came as though it were the first time in a month. Ounce after ounce of cum splattered Harry's insides. When Cleve pulled out, the floor got more buttery than a popcorn cart after an explosion.

5

BANANA HAMMOCK

Cleve artfully lifted Mike's key for the shack when he picked up his pants. The shift had gone into double overtime; it was time for everyone to go home. Mike was too tired to notice the missing key. Cleve cleaned the floor with a dirty rag and threw it in the wastebasket. He shut the door tight behind them and ensured the master lock had snapped closed. That way, Mike wouldn't have to get out his key for any reason.

The Santa Cruz city bus had stopped running. It was several miles uphill to campus.

Mike said to Harry, "Do you want a ride?"

Cleve interrupted. "I already offered him one." He hadn't, but Harry was relieved to ride with Cleve. Mike was nice, but he was 7 out of 10. Cleve was an eleven. Just sniffing the musk coming from his underarms made Harry swoon. A car ride with the muscular security guard sounded like heaven.

Cleve's car was an extension of his muscular frame. It was a Chevy Camaro with leather seats. The exterior was buffed and primed for a paint job, but it looked like it had been that way for a while.

Cleve said, "I'm saving up to paint it red."

"You'll get pulled over more often."

"Not as often as when it's all janky like this."

Harry chuckled. "Is she fast?"

"Does a bear shit in the woods?" Cleve fired up the transmission and gunned it. The car let out a roar that was a few decibels shy of a sonic boom.

"Get in! I'll show you what she can do."

The road to campus, Bay Drive, was a windy uphill climb on a two-lane road. Cleve took the road at twice the speed limit. Harry gripped the oh-shit handle with both hands. Cleve laughed.

"Shall I go faster?"

Harry shook his head, feeling ill. "There's cops patrolling the gate, so you might want to..."

Cleve slammed on the brakes and brought the car close to the speed limit. They sailed onto campus past the flying IUD and pulled into the one-hour parking spot.

Harry pecked Cleve on the cheek. "Thanks, Cleve."

"Can I see your place?"

Harry felt three worlds melting together. His work life, his sex life, and his campus life were coalescing with Cleve's question.

An angel on his shoulder whispered, "Fuck it."

Harry said, "My roommate Forrest might be home. He's an Evangelical Christian."

"I'll behave."

Harry shrugged and said, "Come on, I'll show you the dorm."

Inside the Porter College Residence hall, a security guard dozed at the desk. Harry held a finger to his lips and they tiptoed past.

Harry lived in a small double on the second floor. He knocked gently to see if Forrest was in. There was no answer.

Harry opened the door cautiously. Forrest was out, probably saving lost souls at a late-night prayer circle.

Harry slept in a hammock that hung above his desk. It was just something he'd done since he was a kid. He couldn't sleep comfortably on a mattress.

"Is this yours?" Cleve sent the empty hammock swinging.

Harry nodded. "Is it a single?"

"Yeah, pretty much. I don't think those hooks would hold the weight of two grown men."

Cleve climbed into the hammock. He lay face down. Harry heard him unbuckle his belt and lower his polyester pants. Through a gap in the hammock, Cleve's monster dong poked through and dangled.

"Suck it."

Harry said, "But, uh, Forrest could walk in any minute."

"Put a sock on the door."

Harry panicked. "He won't know what that means. He's a born-again Christian."

Cleve's cock had swollen and stretched to its full size. It was stiff and thick, and a dribble of pre-cum landed on the desk below. "You'd better get me off quick, then."

Harry gave up. He was hypnotized by the fat meat swinging back and forth in the hammock. He sat on the desk and put the huge cock in his mouth. He was sore from earlier, but he opened wide and pushed hard. The thick head forced its way past his tonsils and into his gullet.

"Mmm yeah! Damn, Harry. Nobody gives head as good as you!"

Harry wrapped his hands around the hammock and planted his hands on Cleve's ass cheeks. He used the leverage to push him even deeper down his throat.

"Yeahhhh! Fuck, boy. Suck my cock!"

The dorm room door opened silently. Neither man noticed that Forrest was back, Bible in hand. The pious student was mute with shock. He gasped silently, watching the sodomy being performed in front of him.

"Let's move to the mattress, Harry, I want to fuck you."

Harry made a noise "Nnnn-n."

Forrest cleared his throat. "That's my mattress."

Cleve nearly fell out of the hammock as he scrambled to cover his nakedness. Harry couldn't even look at his roommate. When he did, he was surprised to see that the religious man had a hand down his pants, stroking himself.

"You can use it, though. If I can join in."

Cleve lay on the mattress, his pole towering high above his hips. Harry sat down on Cleve's cock, still slippery from the deep throating it got earlier. When Harry was fully impaled, he unbuttoned his roommate's suit pants. "You want me to suck it?"

Forrest nodded. "The Lord won't mind."

Harry was relieved that soft, Forrest was just a little bigger than average. As the Bible-thumper got erect, however, his cock doubled and redoubled in length and thickness. It was a huge fat cock like Cleve's. Maybe not as thick, but at least as long. It was much easier to swallow because the girth was reasonable. But it reached well past the tonsils and punched some spot deep in Harry's throat. Harry gagged and pulled back. Forrest shook his head and grabbed Harry by the ears, pulling him the rest of the way down. "Suck it, faggot."

Cleve said, "Watch it, Bible boy. We're all faggots here."

Forrest leaned over and held Cleve's head in his hands. He kissed him. "Sorry, bad habit. I'm trying to be more tolerant."

Cleve smiled. "I'll show you tolerance when I'm done with Harry."

Harry used his thigh muscles to ride up and down on Cleve's cock. Each time he sat down, the head made that exhilarating trip around the corner into his colon. He quickly realized that if he could do it fast enough, it would bring his insides to orgasm. He took long strokes on Cleve's cock, and even longer strokes on Forrest's massive cock. He was the lucky Pierre, jammed full at both ends. Cleve leaned around and watched as Harry thoroughly inhaled the full length of Forrest.

"He's talented."

Forrest nodded. "My girlfriend doesn't go past the tip."

Harry felt proud. He was acclimated to Cleve's huge cock in his ass, and now he was an expert cock-sucker to boot.

Harry finally triggered the muscular contractions in his gut that would bring Cleve to orgasm. "It's happening."

"Oh shit! How do you do that? It's like you're squeezing me from deep inside! Oh, fuck! Oh, here it comes!" Cleve unloaded another slippery load of cum inside Harry. As tended to happen, the cum found its way out in a fine spray around the edges of Cleve's cock.

Forrest saw the cum back-spatter escaping Harry's asshole. "Oh, sweet Jesus. Oh, that's good."

Deep in Harry's throat, Forrest unleashed a month's supply of sperm. Harry coughed and gagged as it filled his throat and some of it spilled into his airway. Forrest pulled his cock out fast, bringing a cupful of the sacred juice with it. Harry coughed until his airway was clear. Cleve rubbed his head.

"That's it. Get it all out." He turned to Forrest. "Now, about that tolerance lesson."

Forrest blanched. "I uh, I've never done that."

Cleve slapped the evangelist's naked ass. "There's always a first time."

Cleve was the art director for the next round of sex. He arranged Harry lying on his back, legs spread in a wide V in the air. He helped Forrest find the hole, which was looser than a belt in a whorehouse. Once Forrest easily snaked his way through Harry's bowels, Cleve came around behind him. There was no Vaseline or other ointment in the room, so Cleve took two squirts of Rose Milk lotion and slathered it on Forrest's behind.

"Oh! It's cold!"

"Just wait, I'll make it hot. Now keep fucking Harry like a good boy."

Forrest's thrusts were half-hearted. His face betrayed real fear.

Even from the strange angle lying on the bed, Harry could see Cleve's cock lined up with Forrest's hole.

"If you relax, it'll feel good." Harry hoped his roommate didn't tighten up at the wrong time. It would hurt.

Cleve arched his back and leaned his hips forward, forcing his cock into Forrest's hole.

"Oh, Jesus! Jesus! Oh man, that hurts!"

Cleve knew how to fuck a man. He stayed right there, where the pain was worst, waiting. Forrest pounded the bed. Harry felt him go soft inside him.

"Get it out! Get thee behind me Satan!"

Cleve laughed. "My dick is a lot of things, but it ain't the devil. Just wait another ten seconds. Count backward."

Forrest counted quickly. By the time he reached one, the expression on his face changed. "Hey, that feels good."

Cleve grabbed Forrest and popped his fat head past the sphincter and rammed it to the back of Forrest's asshole.

Forrest jumped, but Harry felt a swelling inside. His roommate was getting hard!

Cleve maneuvered so that his huge cock could push past the rectum into the colon. With a loud pop, he entered the promised land.

Harry was astonished at how much Forrest was growing inside him. Taking a cue from Cleve, the biblical scholar turned his cock so it could pass out of Harry's rectum. Forrest's hips collided with Harry's pale ass cheeks. Harry pulled them apart and let Forrest in all the way. Cleve's thrusts were growing so powerful, they traveled. Harry recognized the pounding rhythm of his hot muscle man passing through Forrest into him. It was fucking by proxy.

Forrest moaned. He was in a state of ecstasy more powerful than any prayer meeting.

"How are you tolerating it, bible boy?" Cleve smirked.

Forrest struggled to find words through the drug-like stupor. "G-good. So good. Divine."

"You're doing good, champ." He held Forrest by the shoulders and drilled in deep. He winked at Harry.

Forrest kept growing inside Harry, stretching him at the seams. It was like Cleve was an air pump and Forrest's cock was a balloon. Each thrust filled Harry more and more.

Cleve reached around and found Harry's pubic mound and nipple-sized cock. It was soaking wet. He rubbed it gently, then more vigorously, until soon Harry was gushing with precum.

Forrest saw the tiny penis dribbling a river of clear semen. He put his hand there, then tasted it.

Between Cleve's fat cock, Harry's slippery hole, and the juicy river of semen, Forrest reached a pinnacle. His eyes fluttered.

"Fuck, I'm gonna come."

Harry had never heard his roommate swear. It was shocking. But true. Forrest must have had a reserve tank of sperm because it felt like he'd emptied a coffee mug inside Harry. Then his body took over. The constant stretching and pounding of his recto-sigmoid junction sent him into an anal orgasm. Muscles contracted, tightening and throbbing against Cleve's girthy cock. To Cleve, it felt like someone had turned on an electric massager.

"Oh shit, Forrest. Keep doing that!"

Forrest said, "I'm not doing it. That's my body. That's you."

Cleve crowed like a rooster before spilling his load in Forrest. It was the fifth time today he had cum, but it was still substantial. Forrest cried aloud when Cleve withdrew quickly. The hole snapped shut, causing Forrest to spasm in waves. He rolled to one side.

Cleve clamped his mouth on Harry's nipple-like penis and tongued it fervently. Harry bucked and moaned and came in Cleve's mouth. Cleve didn't stop. He kept licking and chewing until Harry came again. Like a woman, Harry kept coming as long as Cleve's tongue worked its magic. Harry had to beg him to stop.

Cleve stuffed his cock down the leg of his pants

and zipped up. He brought the two men to him and they kissed as a group. Dicks got hard, and some got wet, but it was so late, they had to stop.

Cleve kissed Harry goodbye and gave Forrest a warm hug. "Welcome to the family."

After Cleve left, Harry turned to his Christian roommate.

"Are you okay?"

Forrest nodded. "Yeah, why?"

Harry frowned. "Was this compatible with your faith?"

Forrest waved a hand in the air. "I got a roommate who does deep throat and lets me ass fuck him. What does faith have to do with it? I'm the luckiest guy in my prayer group!"

"You don't plan to tell them?"

"Only the ones I know are looking for a guy like you."

6

PRAYER CIRCLE

When Harry got back from class the next day, there were three men, including Forrest, sitting in a circle in the middle of the dorm room floor. Forrest smiled.

"Harry, this is Karl Sawyer and Amos Williams. Guys, this is my roommate Harry I was telling you about."

The men grinned. Karl spoke in a deep voice. "Join our prayer circle, Harry."

Harry put his book bag down on his desk. "I'm not much of a praying type."

Amos chuckled. "I hear you're down on your knees praising the Lord's creations all the time."

Forrest hadn't been kidding. These two were not here to save Harry's soul. They were here to invade his hole.

Harry sat between Karl and Amos. They had their pants unzipped; their cocks were hiding under their shirts. By the looks of it, Forrest was the smallest of the three. Amos had a massive lump just above his belly button. Karl had something protruding from between his pectoral muscles. These guys were monsters!

"Wh-what did you wanna pray about?"

Amos lifted his shirt, letting a very thick eight-incher fall onto his thigh. "I need release. Let's pray on it."

Karl put his palm near the top of his chest, almost to the collar of his shirt, and rubbed vigorously. "I'm in need of the same."

Amos said, "I hear you were able to suck Forrest better than his girlfriend. Can I try?"

He lifted his extremely girthy meat from his thigh. Harry hadn't blown anyone so thick before. "I'm not sure it'll fit in my mouth."

Amos looked crestfallen. Harry felt bad.

"Let me try." Harry leaned to the side and stretched out, putting the tip of the fat beast in his mouth. His plump bottom strained against his jeans. He felt strong hands on his waistband. Karl pulled Harry's jeans down to his knees.

Harry held Amos's fat cock in one hand. The fingers didn't reach. He turned his head to see Karl's eleven-inch cock flop down from under the t-shirt. It was a huge, uncut slab of meat. It throbbed with lust. Karl spat in his hand and slicked it up.

Harry turned his attention back to Amos, who was getting thicker with each passing moment. Harry stretched his mouth wide, hoping his teeth wouldn't scrape. He forced the head all the way into his mouth and into the back of his throat. He gagged and swallowed, forcing Amos deeper. It felt like he was taking a whole bottle of pills at once. His throat swelled as Amos moved in.

"Holy cow, Harry!" Amos was astounded.

It was just then that Harry felt a slippery hand at his asshole. It was Karl, stretching him with his fingers. Harry turned to look. He gasped. Karl had grown beyond the length of a ruler. It looked thin, but only because it was so long. Karl was nearly as thick as Amos.

Karl didn't ask permission, nor did he show any mercy when he invaded Harry's shitter. He pressed in and forced his way without pausing until he'd popped past the inner hole. His pubic hairs tickled Harry's bottom. The pain was intense, but Harry had learned to love that feeling. It was a strange mixture of sensations and thoughts. He felt useful. He felt full. He wanted to be of service to a man as big as Karl, whose girlfriend would probably never let him fuck her. How would Karl ever have children with such a monster? He had to. The world needed more men with cocks like Karl's.

Harry was nearly blue. He'd been so busy thinking about Karl's huge cock that he'd forgotten he had Amos lodged deep in his esophagus, blocking his access to oxygen. He pulled back, took a massive breath, and went back down.

"Oh, my Lord." Amos threw his head back and moaned. Harry was making his dreams come true.

Karl pulled out of Harry, only to plunge the entire length all the way back in. Harry would cry out, but he couldn't. Not with Amos blocking him.

Forrest stood beside Amos. The next time Harry came up for breath, he held Amos aloft and went down on Forrest. Yesterday he'd thought his roommate was pretty huge. He was not as long and not as thick as Amos, so going down on him was a breeze. Harry alternated between the two men.

Behind him, Karl was a battering ram. Although nothing held a candle to Cleve, Karl was still a brutal invading army. His thrusts were rough and long. Harry felt the twinge of anal orgasm beginning. Karl's steady rhythm brought it on.

"What's that?" Karl felt the vibrations, like a humming against his cock.

Harry took a breath. "I'm cumming inside."

Karl smiled. "I did that, huh?"

Harry nodded, his mouth full of Amos's monster cock.

The twitching and spasming grew more intense. Harry's throat had opened enough to allow him to go all the way down on one man, then all the way down on the other in rapid succession. He trembled as Karl snaked his way through his guts.

Amos released some salty precum. Harry looked up into his eyes, and Amos nodded. Harry took the beast out of his mouth and sucked on Forrest. He jerked Amos's heavy cock.

Amos shuddered. "Oh shoot. Oh no. I'm going to come."

Harry released Forrest, jerking both men with equal vigor. He put his tongue to Amos's cock head and licked. It fired a massive round of white paste on Harry's face. Then it repeated, a dozen times until Harry was covered in Amos's reproductive fluids. Forrest couldn't hold it. He shot a series of massive loads in Harry's eyes, ears, mouth, and hair. Harry looked like an iced cupcake. He licked the sticky cum from around his mouth, then wiped as much as he could, licking his hands to clean them.

The whole time this was happening, his guts were churning around Karl's long fat cock. Karl was covered in sweat, punching his way into Harry with long, fast strokes.

Harry buried his head in his arms and moaned. Every few strokes, Karl missed the second hole and punched Harry's rectum hard. Harry felt droplets of pee escaping his tiny penis. He was afraid he would wet the floor but Karl took a long, hard stroke, all the way inside Harry. Harry spread his cheeks to let him push even further.

"Yes! Oh, holy Jesus yes!"

A warm flood of Christian jism filled Harry's colon. Karl collapsed on top of Harry, holding him tightly in his arms. Harry was a little surprised when Karl kissed his ear and whispered, "Jesus loves you."

Forrest handed out washcloths. Amos wiped the tip of his cock clean. Harry's washcloth got soaking wet wiping off the two loads of cum from his face. Karl wiped the sweat from his face and body. He was still wedged deep inside Harry.

"I think I'm stuck, man. I gotta go again."

Harry smiled. "I didn't come yet. Go ahead."

While Karl fucked him a second time, Harry took his penis between thumb and forefinger and rubbed on it. He placed the washcloth underneath. With Karl giving his insides another historical pounding, it didn't take long for Harry to shoot his load. Most of it overshot the washcloth, landing on the nearby furniture and rug. His cock was a fraction of the size of these men, but he came as much if not more than any of them.

Karl saw the rocket of cum flying across the room. "Oh man, that's so much. Where do you keep it all?"

Harry shrugged.

Karl plugged away for ten minutes, then fifteen. Harry's ass was raw. It was numb from all the fucking, but he knew it was going to hurt later. At last, Karl reached his second orgasm. Another warm shower sprayed his insides. Harry sighed with relief. Karl pulled out, leaving a bloody pool of cum on the floor.

Then the strangest thing happened. Karl vomited.

Amos held him. "What's wrong?"

Karl shivered. "I can't believe how disgusting that was. I'm a disgrace to God."

Forrest said, "Chill, brah. It's not a sin."

Karl stuffed his monster back in his pants, zipped up, and ran from the room. Amos ran after him.

Forrest shook his head. "Sorry, Harry. Some Christians are a little conflicted, that's all."

Harry got paper towels to clean up the mess Karl left. He felt uncomfortable knowing he'd made the man puke. But it was nothing to the discomfort he felt when he tried to walk across the room.

Forrest pointed to his leg. "You're bleeding out your ass."

Harry felt faint. Every step was agony. "I gotta go to the infirmary."

Harry put an arm around Forrest and his roommate flagged down a security guard in a golf cart. "My roommate needs to go to the infirmary."

Harry remembered getting into the cart.

The next thing he remembered was waking up in an ambulance.

"Where am I?"

The handsome paramedic said, "You lost a lot of blood, man. You're going to the hospital."

Harry frowned. "But it was just sex."

The paramedic laughed. "You better tell him to change his technique. He nearly killed you."

Harry felt a painful throbbing in his guts. "It really hurts."

The paramedic smiled. "This should help." He injected something into the saline bag and everything went white.

7

DOCTOR'S ORDERS

Harry was lying in a recovery room when next he awoke. He looked around the room and through the blur made out a figure in a chair, half asleep.

"Cleve?"

Cleve jumped to his feet and rushed to Harry's bedside. "Oh man, I'm so glad you're okay."

"How did you find me?"

"When you missed your shift, I went to see Forrest. He told me what happened. I'm so sorry. I shouldn't have been so rough."

Harry was confused. Karl was rough. Not Cleve. Then he thought about what Forrest might have said in the circumstances. He'd let Cleve think it was his doing.

"Forrest didn't tell you the whole story."

Cleve frowned. "I don't follow."

Harry told him about the "prayer circle" and Karl's abusive fucking. He thought Cleve would be pissed with him. He wasn't.

"I'll kill that fucker. Where does he live? Is he on campus?"

Harry sighed wearily. "I'm sorry, Cleve. I cheated. It's my fault."

"What? No, shut up about that, Harry. We aren't going steady yet."

"Yet?" Harry smiled weakly. "Are you asking me out, Cleve?"

The security guard blushed. "If it will keep you safe, then yes. If some guy is going to put you in the hospital, it'd better be me."

Harry laughed.

Cleve smiled. "That didn't come out right. Harry Shore, will you be my boyfriend?"

"Yes. I will."

The doctor came into the room, looking suspiciously at Cleve. "Your, uh, brother here says he's your closest family."

"I'm adopted. Yes. Cleve's my brother."

The doctor looked at Cleve's bulging pant leg. "I'm not sure what's going on here, but I think this man, your so-called brother, put you in the hospital with that...thing."

Cleve's hands became fists. A vein popped out on his neck. Harry put a hand on his waist. "It's okay, Cleve. Let me."

Cleve backed down.

Harry said, "I can see how you might think that, but the guy who did this wasn't half as talented as Cleve."

The doctor blushed. "I didn't mean to...well, I am just hoping to protect you from further injury, son."

"The guy who did this is never coming near me again."

"Do you want to report a rape?"

Harry took a deep breath to regain his patience. "It

wasn't rape. It was a careless accident. Karl is inexperienced."

The doctor raised an eyebrow. That was when Harry saw his name tag. It read 'Dr. Sawyer." That was Karl's last name!

"You say this happened on campus?"

Harry was annoyed with the doctor. He started to play with him. "Yeah, oddly enough it was at a prayer circle."

The doctor dropped his clipboard. He glared at Harry when he picked it up.

Harry kept at it. "Karl is big. Really big. Not like Cleve, but almost. And he's not used to fucking. I think he gets turned down a lot because of his, uh, thing."

The doctor unbuttoned his top collar and wiped the sweat from his forehead. "Okay, I get the picture."

Cleve interrupted. "When can we do it again?"

The doctor said, "The stitches need a few days to heal and dissolve before anything else can go up... there. Nothing before this weekend."

Cleve sighed. "Thank you, doc."

The doctor said, "I don't normally share this, but it seems fair to you two that I do. I have seen this type of problem before. My wife can't take me, and so I find my relief with men." He grabbed his pant leg, revealing a monster hanging halfway to his knee. "I know that you figured out Karl is my son. He's my only son. I put my wife in the hospital on our honeymoon. It's a miracle she gave birth at all. And she'll never have children again."

Harry leaned on one elbow to prop himself up, painfully.

Cleve nodded. "So you can relate."

The doctor said, "It's a strange club. I'm glad I'm a

member, but it's not easy. Harry will never know the troubles we see."

Harry said, "I see the troubles you have, though!"

The doctor smiled. "When Karl hit puberty, his problems became like yours and mine." He nodded at Cleve. "I'm afraid I told him too much. He's angry with God for making him too big for women. I'm sorry you had to suffer, Harry."

Harry shrugged. "He was rough, but I liked it."

Dr. Sawyer frowned. "He was too rough. He needs to be taught."

Harry said, "Well, Cleve's a pretty good teacher."

And a plan was hatched.

8

____

A VERY BIG LESSON

That weekend, Dr. Sawyer invited Cleve and Harry to his house for Sunday lunch. Mrs. Sawyer prepared a roast with all the trimmings. Cleve and Harry were sitting in the living room when Karl walked in. He balled up his fists and hissed at Harry. "What the fuck are you doing here?'

Cleve stood up and put a hand on Karl's shoulder. "Easy there, son. We're guests."

Dr. Sawyer came in. "Karl, this is Cleve. And I hear you had the pleasure of meeting Harry already."

"Dad, what is this?"

The doctor handed Karl a rocks glass filled with ice and single-malt whisky. "Have a drink. This talk is long overdue."

Karl's fists relaxed. He took the glass from his father and sat in an overstuffed chair, glaring at Harry.

"I've invited Cleve and Harry for your benefit."

"You're going to hell, Dad. For being a fucking fag."

The Doctor smiled. "After your mother leaves for her quilting bee, we'll continue the discussion."

Dinner was delicious. Harry wondered if Mrs. Sawyer knew the purpose of their visit. If she did, she wasn't perturbed. After the roast, she served butterscotch pudding for dessert. She grabbed her purse.

"I'm off to quilt. You boys have fun. She winked at Harry."

No sooner was the door closed than the Doctor smacked Karl across the face.

"Don't you ever call anyone a faggot, son. It's disgraceful. What would Jesus say? For one thing, you yourself have partaken in sex with men."

"I ain't got no other choice. That don't make me a faggot. You and these guys do it because you like it."

Harry chimed in. "I have a hard time believing you didn't like being with me."

Karl sneered but said nothing.

Dr. Sawyer said, "Leave your judgment at the door, Karl. We're part of God's design. He made us this way and it's our job to enjoy what he gave us."

Karl sighed. "Why did you invite these two fruit—I mean fellows over here? Is this some weird kinky sex thing?"

"Karl, I spent two hours stitching this boy up last week because someone was too rough with him. Too big and too rough."

Karl stared at the rug.

"You need to learn how to use your gift. I asked Cleve to show you. He's bigger than either of us, but he's gentle and strong."

Karl covered his reddening face with his big hands.

"I think I'm going to die of embarrassment. Dad, you're a creep and a freak."

Cleve stood next to Karl and put a hand on his shoulder. "Trust me, the birds and the bees are enough for most guys. We need extra instruction to learn how to handle ourselves."

Karl softened his shoulders at Cleve's touch. "Who taught you?"

Cleve smiled. "My uncle. He was a legend."

Something subtle changed in the room. There was a slight scent of musk as the four men transmitted airborne signals of lust. Harry, the most sensitive of the four men, shifted in his chair. His ass was quivering with desire.

Dr. Sawyer unfastened the top button of his shirt, loosening his tie. Karl released the last of his defiance in submission to Cleve. His eyes traveled down, down, down growing wider as he searched for the end of Cleve's cock. Cleve's double-knit polyester pants strained to contain the roaring hardon that was increasing in length and girth down his leg.

"You're not fucking me with that, are you?" Karl meant it as a question, but it came out as a request.

Cleve leaned forward and whispered in Karl's ear. "I'll be gentle. You'll see." He nibbled on Karl's earlobe, which sent the younger man into paroxysms of pleasure. Harry watched as Cleve expertly guided his prey to the plaid sofa. Karl gasped when Cleve pulled on his pants. They slid down to his knees, releasing the gargantuan cock that had brutalized Harry just a week earlier.

Cleve lifted Karl's knees towards his ears, exposing his pink hole. Just as he'd done with Harry under the boardwalk, Cleve used his tongue to tease pleasure from fear. Karl wriggled and gave a satisfied moan. Cleve reached into his pocket and pulled out a travel-sized tub of Vaseline. He dipped his finger, then inserted it in Karl's anus.

Watching from his armchair, Harry felt a fatherly hand on his shoulder. He touched his cheek to the Doctor's hand, rubbing like a kitten marking its territory. The doctor responded by holding Harry's head to his crotch. Harry could feel the doctor throbbing in his pants. He traced the cock with his hand until he reached the tip. It was impressive, perhaps even bigger than Karl. But of course, nothing compared to Cleve.

On the couch, Karl kicked off his jeans so he could hold his ankles apart.

"Oh, sweet Jesus that feels good." He'd probably never had a lubed finger in his ass before. Harry could almost see Karl taking a mental note to do this with his next partner. Cleve added a second finger. Karl sucked air between his teeth.

"Relax, buddy. Let me take care of everything."

Karl nodded. His eyes fluttered as he laid his head on the couch cushion and let Cleve work his magic. He didn't appear to notice when Cleve got a third finger in there. The furry muscleman was a smooth operator.

When Cleve spread his fingers, Harry saw right into Karl's shiny pink hole. Karl chewed a finger.

"Am I hurting you, Karl?"

The prayer leader shook his head vigorously.

"Are you ready for the tip?"

He nodded with equal vigor. A panicked expression crossed his face when Cleve shucked his pants.

"Shush. Don't worry. I'm an expert." Cleve reassured Karl by stroking the boy's cock, which had shriveled from fear. It rose to attention once more.

Harry felt movement by his shoulder. The doctor was standing, stroking his massive cock, watching his son lose his anal virginity.

Cleve wielded his cock with two hands, steadying it as it found the pink pathway to Karl's guts. He pressed gently, allowing half the head to enter.

"When you fuck, do you wait like this?"

Karl shook his head.

"Wait right here like I'm doing, okay? You gotta give the guy or girl a chance to mentally prepare for what's coming."

Karl understood. "Yes, sir."

Cleve leaned in, forcing the huge head most of the way in. Karl pounded the sofa.

"Fuck! Ow! It's too big!"

Cleve smiled. "Count to ten. On the count of ten, I'll push in further."

Karl began counting. At seven, Cleve popped the corona past the sphincter and lunged forward. He stopped and waited.

Karl's face was screwed up with pain. "You said ten!"

Cleve grinned. "Start over. Count to ten. I promise I won't move a muscle."

Cleve kept his promise. By the time Karl reached ten, his face relaxed. Cleve pulled back an inch or two and moved forward just a little more. Karl's eyes grew wide.

"Why does it feel so good?"

Cleve shrugged. "I'm an expert, what can I say?"

Harry watched fascinated. Cleve's technique was working on this uptight bible thumping freshman. Dr. Sawyer was just as amazed. He turned to Harry.

"Your boyfriend is performing a miracle right before our eyes."

Harry said, "Watching it all is amazing. I feel a bit left out."

The doctor smiled. "Do you want to sit on my lap to watch the show?"

"I thought you'd never ask."

The show was moving along quickly. The loud gasp was a sign that Cleve had popped through the second hole into the deep recesses of Karl's bowels. At long last, Cleve's hips connected with Karl's thighs. Both men let out a heavy breath.

"You ready to find paradise?"

Karl shook his head. "I'm already there. Go for it."

Cleve pulled back, causing Karl to jump as the fat head left the second hole. He rammed forward, making an audible pop as he plunged back through. He picked up speed, forcing his cock in and out of that hole over and over. Karl's moans filled the room. His cock stood at full attention, reminding Harry of the huge cock hanging beside him.

Harry stood and let Dr. Sawyer sit in the recliner. He lowered himself onto the doctor's massive lubed cock, feeling it slide inside his entrails. Harry bounced in time to Cleve's thrusts, making the show come to life for both him and the doctor. Cleve changed patterns frequently, making Harry's job even more challenging.

The luckiest man in the room was Karl. He was getting a world-class fuck while learning the correct technique for fucking with his massive tool. What better way to learn fucking than to be expertly fucked?

Harry accepted that his tiny tool would never be used for fucking. Hearing the satisfied moans of the doctor beneath him made him proud of his beautiful ass. Karl's ass was flat. He was built for fucking, not for being fucked. But Cleve made it look otherwise. Karl howled and whined like a girl, his ass split open by Cleve's huge hog.

Harry's bouncing had brought the doctor too far along. Manly hands held his bottom. "Don't. Stop. You're gonna make me cum."

Harry stopped, feeling the doctor's huge member throbbing inside him, on the cusp of orgasm.

The doctor made a sound like a yawn. "I'm gonna cum. Don't stop."

Harry bent his knees and straightened them four or five times in rapid succession. His bottom filled with a warm flood of cum. The doctor said, "Holy shit. You're good."

Harry smiled to himself. The doctor hadn't even scratched the surface of Harry's talents. He stood, letting the softening cock flop out of him. He held his rectum tight, savoring the warmth of the semen in his belly.

Karl was in ecstasy. He thrashed on the couch. His eyes caught Harry's. "Come here."

Harry left the doctor in his post-coital bliss and let Karl touch his tiny genitals.

"They're so pretty. I wish I had a little one like you."

Harry shrugged. He hardened in Karl's meaty fingers, drooling a little precum on his hand. He reached out and stroked Karl's big log. Karl's eyes pleaded with him. Silently, he asked Harry to sit on his cock.

With Cleve plugging away from below, Harry straddled Karl's chest and lowered himself onto the huge cock. The doctor's cum still inside him made a perfectly smooth lubricant. Karl held his bottom, lowering and lifting him in time to Cleve's thrusts. Like an electrical circuit, the energy of Cleve's fucking passed through Karl's ass, into Karl's cock, and then into Harry's ass. The transfer of energy made Harry's hard little cock throb. He shot a load all over Cleve's face and chest. Karl got a little on his thighs.

Cleve licked his lips to clean them. He said to Karl, "Do you know how to fuck now, boy?"

Karl said, "Yes, sir."

Cleve said, "Good. Help me fuck Harry."

Cleve pulled his cock out of Karl and pressed it up to Harry's already stuffed hole. He pushed hard. Harry's ass felt like it was being torn apart, but it held. He could smell Karl's ass on Cleve's dick. It made him hard again. Cleve shoved his way in beside Karl.

"You need to feel the rhythm of my cock next to yours."

Karl nodded. Cleve took Karl's hands off Harry's bottom. Harry rolled onto Karl's chest, his knees by his ears. Cleve pushed until he was all the way inside. Harry had never felt this full before. He wondered if he would be able to go back to just one dick inside him after this!

The doctor stood over his son, his cock hanging to his lips. Karl took his dad in his mouth and sucked, gagging as the doctor knelt lower.

Cleve fucked Harry just right. Karl was not able to thrust, being underneath, but the friction of Cleve's thrusts made up for it. Harry felt that strange rush of pleasure that preceded spasms. His ass throbbed, squeezing and caressing the two dicks inside him.

"Mmmnf!" Karl's mouth was full; he tried to express his surprise at the sensation of Harry clamping down on his cock while Cleve rubbed against him with his club-like monster.

Harry's toes curled. "Oh, Jesus. Oh, God." It was enough to give him a second orgasm. The air filled with his cum, splattering everyone and everything in its path.

Seeing Harry cum without hands put Cleve at the zenith. "Oh fuck, I did it again." He pounded the boy's ass, careful not to damage him.

Karl made more noises. His father was fucking his face. He thrashed and twisted. It was all too much. He came inside Harry, coating Cleve's cock with his young dumb cum.

Cleve closed his eyes. "Ooh yeah." He cut loose a flood of warm cum deep in Harry's entrails. The two huge cocks were slippery and wet with three loads of cum.

Karl gagged and slurped his father's load. Everyone was satisfied. The evening had been a success.

EPILOGUE

On the ride home, Harry recalled something the doctor had said.

"Cleve, Doctor Sawyer called you my boyfriend."

Cleve concentrated on the road. "Uh-huh."

Harry let the silence persist. He felt something for Cleve that he'd never felt before. His rational mind struggled with his heart. Cleve was a security guard. Harry was in college. What could the two of them talk about besides sex?

Cleve broke the silence. "Do you want to be boyfriends?"

Harry's heart spoke first. "Yes. Yes, I do."

Cleve grinned. "Good. Me too."

Throughout the season, Cleve and Harry met nightly in the shack under the roller-coaster. Cleve found a hundred ways to bring Harry to orgasm. When the boardwalk switched to winter hours, Cleve was promoted to deputy chief of security. With the new salary, he could afford to rent a small bungalow downtown. Harry moved in with him. Not only did it make sense financially, but it was also the next step in their relationship. If they lived in a different world, they probably would have been married in the springtime. But that world is just a dream for now.

The End

DORMITORY URGES

by Chuck Idgaf

DORMITORY URGES

It's the early 90s, and I'm a junior in college. I just started at a four-year university after going to community college. I'm avoiding coming to terms with my sexuality. I have only recently lost my virginity to a girl a few months earlier and am now sexually active with the girl I'm currently dating.

Here's the catch: I've been jerking off to thoughts and images of men since junior high. But the types of men that I find attractive are not what you'd think of when someone says "gay." Then, I've had pleasurable sex with both of these women, not really understanding that sexuality is a scale and when you're 20, sometimes, any hole will do. Not to mention, both of these girls have gay friends who really complicate things for me. They claim that bisexuality isn't real, a typical 90s attitude. Also, their attitude is that only twinks matter and everyone else in a gay bar is a troll. Needless to say, I just dig deeper into my hole of self-loathing, thinking I just have some weird fetish. I guess I should explain that.

My junior high band director had been a power-lifter in his younger days. He was a tall, large, BROAD man who had succumbed to middle age with a good-sized belly. He had a mostly bald head and a tuft of soft fur peeking through the open collar from his ubiquitous polo shirts. His nipples could always be seen, even in winter, through an additional sweater layer, the size of a large pencil eraser like the ones you used in kindergarten. His areolae were as large as a half-dollar coin at least, with hair sprouting out around them, which could be seen through his thin polo shirts. He was the center of my early jack-off fantasies. They expanded to friends, fathers, men at church, and other teachers. But always around a theme. Hairy. The hairier, the better. A big belly. From full-on beer gut to a small paunch above the belt – as long as they weren't fit. Definitely not muscled. Bald was good, too, which seemed to go along with hairy in most cases, but it wasn't required. Sciency and smart were also attractive, maybe a touch nerdy. But macho was a turn-off. A lot of the coaches in high school were physically hot, but they were such dicks that they never entered the spank bank. Anyway, I felt like these physical qualities, coupled with kindness and compassion, were what made a man manly and me horny.

Hollywood films of the '70s and '80s only featured implied gays, all of whom were slim and fit, bleach blonde, and nelly. So I just assumed I couldn't be gay because that didn't turn me on at all. I never took the chance to look at my classmates in the locker room. Never cared. Late teens, in college, I had the opportunity to see the first girl's gay friend's cock. It was interesting to see one in person, but I didn't want to do anything with it. It was attached to someone my age. All this just reaffirmed I wasn't gay. Also, he was slightly above average, reaffirming my long-standing fear of being small. I'd seen my father's a few times, and it was notable, even limp. I didn't inherit those genes. (I did get great body hair from my mom's side, but that didn't come in until almost 30).

So now I'm on campus at a university, and at least I'm not a virgin anymore. That helps my angst a little. Maybe I should tell you a bit about how I look. 6'2", maybe 150 pounds. Scrawny is the word I would use. That tall with a 28" waist on a good day. No muscle; I'm mostly a nerd. Not a completely awkward geek, but the smart, shy type. Average looks, but not a head-turner. My cock is cut and on the lower end of average. About a roll of quarters thick and just under 6" on a good day. My balls are also on the small side and always drawn up tight, retreating uncomfortably inside from time to time.

One evening, I'm walking to the caf for dinner before they closed, and there's two large, nerdy guys sitting outside the next dorm having a chat. They're my age, so I don't really notice them. The one I can see isn't my type. Sort of too much of a good thing is then a bad thing. Taller than me. Big belly, almost too big. I like the fold a belly makes when it hangs. I want to rub my hand under there while I spoon a guy from the back. Once there's no waist, it doesn't turn me on anymore. This guy's belly is on the cusp, if not over it sizewise. As I walk past, I turn to both of them to politely nod hello. I almost trip while doing a double take of the other guy, whose back was to me until that moment. Holy Fuck, I've never seen a boy my age who has so much as given me a tingle, let alone the instant boner that now strains uncomfortably in my jeans.

He's a little shorter than me, maybe 5'10". Broad, but not like my old band director. Broad, not from working out, just bone structure, and he's on the chunky side. His belly is perfect. It's just starting to roll over his belt buckle. It's big enough that hugging him from behind, my hands would just be able to overlap. Brown hair with sandy streaks, perfectly cut and combed as if his parents had raised him in a perfect "Leave it to Beaver" family, and he couldn't leave the house unkempt. He's clean-shaven, but his end-of-day stubble hints he'd be hairy. The smile on his adorable face is disarming, accentuated by his slightly chubby chipmunk cheeks. His gentle eyes twinkle as he smiles. His brown plaid short-sleeve shirt is pressed and neatly tucked in, accenting his belly. Every button except the top buttoned, just a hint of thick brown fur almost peeking out. His khaki shorts reveal stocky but strong calves covered in a dusting of short, soft brown hair. As he turns to nod hello back, I can make out the outline of his cock down his inner right thigh. They're loose enough that there isn't a lot of detail but enough to make it look like he's sneaking a beer can into a movie theater.

His image plays in slow motion over and over as I eat dinner. I replay it repeatedly, wondering how I might have broken the ice. I doubt he's even gay. I'd never even played with a cock; what would I do with one that big? Was it an optical illusion? How inferior would I feel if I actually got to see it? So many thoughts are running through my mind. I finish dinner and walk back the way I came to see if they're still there. They're gone. I realize I have no idea how to find him. I don't even know his name. I've been at school for a few months, and that was the first time I've seen him on a giant campus. I doubt I'll see him again. I return to my room. And spunk the biggest load I've ever shot.

Spring semester has come, and nothing much has changed in my life. I have a couple of new profs in the spank bank now, but that's about it. One day, I get a form letter about yearbooks being available. Who knew colleges had yearbooks? I didn't. I didn't even realize that I could have had a picture made. Guess they were less diligent about getting out that message. Plus, like I said, I mostly leave campus in my free time for my girlfriend. I wonder what else I'd missed on campus. Anyway, I think, "What the heck. It's free," and go to get one at the campus bookstore.

I spot a couple of people I know in the yearbook, but I don't feel too bad about not being in it, as most of the people in my classes aren't in there either. Then, I do a double take. There he is! Ryan. I have a name. I scour the yearbook to see if he's in any activities or clubs. Nothing. Oh well. At least I have a tiny picture of his face to spank to on occasion.

I turn 21 that semester. I also get my dream job, well, part-time dream job, that is. Record store at the mall. The assistant manager is interesting. Late 20s. Plays in a band that's pretty well-known in the surrounding states. He rallies a few of us to go out after work sometimes. It's enough to get me out of my wallflower state and into joining them more often than not. One night, we get to the bar, and the weekly trivia match is still going. I notice a really tall guy with one of the groups playing. It's Ryan's friend from the stoop outside the dorms. I quickly scan the rest of the group, but no one looks anything like him. Bummer. I go to the bar to order. As I walk up to the bar, I see a guy just getting his order and turning to walk away. He almost bumps into me. It's him! He's even cuter than I remembered. And now he has a beard. A young man's beard. Trimmed down on the cutes. Soft, brown hair. But damn, a sexy, manly beard nonetheless. He stops short, nearly spilling his drinks. "Oh. Sorry."

"No worries," I say, "my bad." Fuck! That smile

again. Before he walks off, my hormones take over, pushing my embarrassment aside, "Have we met before?"

"You do look familiar."

"Maybe we've just seen each other on campus."

He says, "I'm in the south hall in the Honors dorm."

"Oh. I'm in the north hall. Maybe that's it."

"I'm Charles," I wave my hand.

He slightly raises his glasses, "I'm Ryan." I swoon inside. He sees my badge from work; I forgot to take it off. "Maybe I've seen you in the store."

I look down at my badge after he nods toward it.

"Possible," I say, knowing it's a fib because I would have remembered him. "Maybe we can hang sometime. Chat about music."

"That'd be great," he says, walking off to his friends at their game table with their beers.

I get my drink, join my group. We get lost in our usual conversation about music, my favorite subject at the time. I don't notice that trivia has ended. Ryan walks up with a fresh beer from the bar, "Mind if I join?" I make introductions, saying we're in the same dorm like we'd known each other awhile. The conversation is great. We all discuss different bands, styles of music we like, and albums we have. We have a few rounds. I'm not drunk, but I have a good buzz. Slowly, folks start to disappear. Ryan and I are the last ones at our table. He says his roommate went home for the weekend and wonders if I'd like to come listen to some of the bands we've been talking about that I didn't know. I don't have any vibe that he's gay or even bi. But I won't be turning down an opportunity to hang out with him. If I get lucky, maybe he'll take off his shirt. Or better sit around in his underwear. The dorms aren't known for the best AC. I follow him back to campus. Parking is easy on the weekends, and we get good spots right between our two halls.

We get to his room. He pops in a cassette. I sit on the small couch, and he sits on his bed, back to the wall. I can just make out the outline of his cock, but realize I should concentrate on the conversation so I don't get a raging erection he can see. We talk about our majors, where we're from, and other friendly small talk. He asks if I have a girlfriend. I say yes and tell him she's at a different school, but we see each other regularly. I ask him the same. He says he had a girlfriend in high school, but she's at community college. He saw her over the holidays but wasn't into it anymore. So I ask if they broke up.

He says, "Not yet. I feel like I don't have a lot of options, but if I'm still not into her over summer break, then I should call it off."

I ask, "What do you mean by 'not a lot of options?' You're a good-looking guy. Is it your size? Some people are into that."

He blushes. I'm not sure if it was because I said he was good-looking or because a guy in general said it.

He says, "I'm shy. It was a fluke that I even dated this girl, to begin with. It was only because she asked me to a Sadie Hawkins dance." He's still flush, but the embarrassment is already out in the open, I guess, because he then doubles down, asking, "So...are you active?"

"Sexually?" I ask.

He nods, face fully red now.

I say, "Yes, we are."

He says, "I'm still a virgin."

"I was, too, until last summer. I think I understand what you're feeling. The 'will it ever happen' feeling."

He nods. I could tell he wanted more.

I say, "I met her, my previous girlfriend, at community college. She gave me blue balls enough that I gave in about all the 'waiting until marriage' stuff I'd been brought up with and let her suck my cock."

He gasps. He's hiding his crotch with a pillow, but I'm sure he's hard because I know I am.

I continue. "Summer was ending, and she was going away to school, and we knew it wouldn't last, so I asked her if she would take my virginity. I didn't say that I was thinking this might be my only chance and I'd better not miss out. I came in three strokes."

We both laugh.

"Cliché, I know. But I did much better the next day. That time, we both came."

He makes a little cheer noise and motion with his hand. I swoon again inside over this cute, nerdy boy.

He says, "That's my fear. That I would have the nerve to ask, and if I do I'll always get turned down. At least she seems interested, and that's better than nothing. But I know that's wrong, and I don't want to be that person. What if I make her miss out on her one person?"

"What a sweet man you are," I think to myself.

He continues, "Plus, look at me. I'm a big guy. And nerdy to boot. Girls aren't dropping like flies for that."

I still have enough of a buzz that I'm feeling brave. "I like that you're honorable. Karma will reward you in the end. Plus, come on, man. You're smokin' hot. I'd do you."

There's an awkward pause. He won't look at me. I can't tell if I've fucked up or not. Is he gonna beat me up? Is he just gonna ignore it? The tension is thick, and time seems to freeze.

Finally, he looks at me and asks, "So, you're bi?"

I shrug. "I like having sex with my girl, but I also fantasize about men. I've never been with a man. Most of the gay guys I've met look like me. Mostly, I find older guys attractive. Guys built like you."

Our eyes are locked on each other. I swallow hard, hoping I haven't just ruined a new friendship by being horny. He looks off to the side, his face red again, scrunched up sheepishly. Without looking at me, he asks, "So...I'd be doing you a favor...if I let you suck my cock?"

I almost come in my pants. I quickly, but not too quickly, counter, "It sounds like we'd be doing each other a favor."

He looks me in the eyes again and nods. "I jerk off at least three times a day. I'm hoping that real sex would give me a little more relief."

I smirk at him and stand up, walking towards him. He gets up and meets me in the middle of the room.

"Where should we start?" he asks.

"Can I kiss you? I've never kissed a man. I'm guessing that's my first test on the bi spectrum."

"Can we stop if I don't like it?"

"Of course."

We awkwardly put our arms around each other. I'll give him credit; he does make a concerted effort. I'm in heaven. The musk of a man. His beard rubbing my face. His big arms wrapped around me. His big belly pushed against me, the heat of this body. Our tongues fighting for dominance in each other's mouths. I don't want it to end, but he pulls away. "It's not really for me," he says.

I'm disappointed, but I do understand. He looks at me like he wants a response. "Oh, I kind of enjoyed it. Your beard feels great."

He blushes but genuinely smiles at the compliment.

We take off our shirts. He's covered in fur. Front and back. I only have a happy trail to a thick bush at this point in my life. I rub his chest fur. "Fuck, dude. I'm so jealous. I'd kill to look like that."

He looks sad. "Not if you were picked on in high school gym."

I say, "Fuck those guys. They were just jealous that you were already a real man, and they were just boys."

His face changes. Just a spark of pride starting.

I say, "I hope I'm not a skinny smooth man. I hope I have sexy fur like that one day."

He blushes again. I rub his belly. I tell him something about it turns me on. He doesn't understand but shrugs and lets me enjoy it a bit. One of his hands hesitantly rubs my smooth chest. He finds a nipple and lightly tweaks it. I inhale with pleasure; he's found one of my spots.

He moves his other hand in and works both nips. He tells me he's jerked off thinking of breasts and playing with every size and shape of nipple. I tell him I've done the same, but both sexes. I make my way up to his nips. They're like I've always imagined my band director's would've been. I'm in heaven.

He says that his nipples don't do anything for him, but he can tell that I like them. I can tell he wants to move on to the good part. I tell him I'm nervous about taking my pants off. I always felt like my cock was smaller than the few others I'd seen, and I'd gotten out of gym in school so I wouldn't be exposed. He encourages me, says it'll be fine, and that he's seen plenty of small ones in the gym.

I have a large wet spot on my shorts already. I remove them. My under 6-inch cock stands straight out.

"That's perfectly normal," he says, "You've got nothing to worry about." He pauses. "Mine isn't exactly normal from what I've seen. Plus, I'm uncircumcised."

"My dad was too, so it won't be the first foreskin I've seen."

He eases a little, but not much. He turns around to remove his shorts. His furry ass sits right in front of me. I want to rub it. He turns back around, and I involuntarily gasp. He turns bright red and looks away.

"I'm so sorry," I say, "It's just so...beautiful." It's rock hard, and the skin still covers all of his head. I can see precum marking the opening. It's about as big around as my wrist but only four-and-a-half inches long, about an inch shorter than mine. (I find out later there's another two inches hidden by his pooge under his belly.) His balls are huge and hang away from his body slightly. I'm enamored and jealous at the same time. He is perfection.

"That's a bit bigger than I expected for my first time," I say, and he blushes again. "I'll do my best, but I'll jerk you off if I can't do it."

He gives a grateful nod.

I motion for him to lay on the bed, and I get between his legs.

First, I lap at the precum with the tip of my tongue. I love eating my own, so I figure I'll be ok with this. It tastes sweet. He moans as the tip of my tongue enters his foreskin. It's filled with thick, sweet precum. I work my tongue around his head, lapping up the sweet nectar. "So far so good," I think, my hesitance lost in a wave of lust. I stroke it a few times, exposing a bit of his shiny head. He moans and moves his hips a little. I pull the skin back, fully exposing his head. I gently wrap my lips around it. It isn't as difficult as I'd thought, but I pay attention to my teeth with this much girth. As soon as I have my lips firmly sealed around the shaft, I know I'm 100% a cocksucker. He gasps as I work my way down the shaft. I enjoy every minute of it. I get it all in my mouth. I push against his pubes and realize that there's more shaft than I'd seen at first. I deep-throat all six-and-a-half inches of it. I fondle his giant nuts. I work up and down the shaft with my other hand. I work my tongue back and forth on the sensitive spot under his head. I pull skin forward, over my tongue and run my tongue round his head in circles.

He loves everything I do, moaning louder with each change. Hard to tell with his big balls, but I feel like they might be tightening some. The sign he's getting close. He grabs my head with both hands and starts to thrust. I like it. He gets deeper and rougher. I can't breathe. I'm getting more turned on and slightly freaking out at the same time. Just when I think I can't take any more, one last deep thrust and then he holds still before letting my head go. A low moan begins to build. I keep my head still. I pull the skin back tight and suck his knob gently, working my tongue around the bottom while slowly stroking the base of his cock. His first shot comes out. I almost choke from the velocity when it hits the back of my throat. Then another and another. I try to swallow them all, but it's so much. It dribbles down my chin. His body spasms with every volley of cum he squirts. I lose count of the number of pulses; they subside eventually. I pull his cock from my mouth, but it's still dribbling cum. He just lays there. I'm not sure if he's passed out or what.

"Are you ok?"

He nods slowly.

I stroke my cock while gently rubbing his belly.

He finally opens his eyes. "That was incredible."

"Not bad for a first-timer," I say.

He sees me stroking my cock and says, "I feel a little guilty...I could try to jerk you off if you want."

My face beams. "That would be great."

He gets some lotion from his roommate's bedside table. He motions for me to lie beside him, facing away from him. I'm on my side, cuddled by this big teddy bear. His fur rubs against my back. The heat of his body soothes me, while his skin against me fuels my desires. He has one arm under me, across my chest. The other arm reaches around and down towards my throbbing cock. He wraps my cock in his thick hand with the lotion on it and begins to stroke. I'm in heaven. His stroke is gentle but firm, just the right pace. I close my eyes and try to focus on being in his arms. I can feel his cock against my ass crack. It's still plump from my blow job.

I feel so tiny with his mass engulfing me. I never knew the excitement I could feel being held by a big man. His other hand rubs my smooth chest a little. I gasp and lightly thrust forward as he grazes my nipple.

"You like that, buddy?" he asks.

I just nod and gasp again as he flicks and twists it gently. The more he plays with it, the more I move my hips. I can feel his cock getting hard again. I push back further, my cheeks spreading. The cum still dribbling from his cock and foreskin makes it slick enough for his cock to slide in and graze my tight hole. I moan as the head rubs against my pucker every time I move my hips. I push back further. Between the calm I feel in his arms and the buzz I still have from the bar, I can tell that his cock is right at the entry point of my hole. Not in, but beginning to stretch. I can feel the slickness of his cum lubing me up. I take a deep breath and push back as I let it out. The massive head slips in. I wince.

"Don't move," I whimper.

My hole is stretched to the limit. It hurts, but I don't want it out. That much is done. I want to see if I can adjust to it. He waits a few seconds, then gently starts to stroke me again. I relax a little more. His cock slowly slides deeper. He takes a long, deep breath as he begins to feel my tight hole engulfing his shaft. "Fu-uuuck," he says, "I've never felt anything like it."

He strokes me faster. He pulls out a bit until just the head is in, and then slowly pushes every inch of his shaft all the way in. I'm being stretched to my limits, and the pressure on my prostate is driving me insane.

He does a few more slow strokes like that, then whispers, "Buddy, I'm gonna need to cum again." He continues to stroke me while fucking my virgin hole. His strokes get faster and shorter, but he's deep inside me. "Fuck, buddy. Can I cum? Can I cum in you?"

"Yes," I say.

He lets go of my cock and grabs my hip. He rolls partially on top of me, pushing me on my belly. His weight on top of me crushes and comforts me at the same time. His arms are wrapped around my chest now. Just his hips move, fucking his cock furiously into my tight hole. He's breathing hard in my ear, whispering non-words, but I know he's in ecstasy. He's trying to tell me he's about to cum. I can tell by his pace, longer, slower, harder thrusts. "I'm cumming." is all he says as he holds his cock all the way deep inside me. The pressure of him on top of me, his full weight as he collapses. The girth of his cock stretching me. The pulsing of his orgasm through his shaft on my prostate. The pressure of another huge load filling, squirting out of my hole around his shaft, dripping down my balls. I begin to cum without touching myself.

"I'm cumming, I'm cumming," I quietly scream over and over. He begins to thrust into me again, rubbing my prostate, forcing every drop of cum out. As my orgasm subsides, he pulls out of me. I can feel my hole gaping open from the abuse it has taken. I'll be sore for sure, but my balls have never been so completely emptied, and the bliss is all I can think about. I pass out, a sticky mess.

The next morning, I wake to find him already up, sitting on the small couch in the room. He looks at me, his eyes sad again. "Thank you for last night. I do feel a little more confident in myself."

I smile and nod. "And thank you. I think I have the answer I was looking for about myself and also a tough conversation in my future, as well."

He nods, knowing what I mean. Then he says, "I don't want to sound ungrateful, and I have no regrets about last night. I don't think I can see you again. I'm not sure how to handle this situation. I'm sorry."

I'm heartbroken. I say, "Our secret."

He smiles as I get up, grab my things and leave. I don't say goodbye so that he won't see the tears in my eyes.

I wish we could have been friends. I'm grateful to him for helping me open the door to a truly happy life. I find him on social media when that becomes a thing. He's gotten married, has kids, and is living what seems like a good life. I don't send a friend request. I'm just glad to know he's found what he was looking for, just like I have.

SLEAZY A

by J. W. Steed

1

TEAROOM EXTRA CREDIT

A boy in an Easter yellow polo shirt occupies the furthermost corner of the campus TV room. He's got the collar popped high around his neck; an Izod alligator logo proudly bares its teeth above his bulging left pec. Pink cardigan hanging around his shoulders, sleeves dangling over his biceps. Pants in pastel blue with little somethings —are they dachshunds?—embroidered all over. And though it's the sunniest and driest of autumn mornings, he's wearing a pair of calf-high L. L. Bean duck boots with untied laces.

Jesus Christ. I bet he picked that outfit while clutching a much-creased copy of *The Official Preppy Handbook*. It's the sacred scripture of this small Southern college. I can tell the guy's girlfriend, giggling in the chair next to him, is a disciple. Of course, she's wearing a ribbon tied in a bow beneath that Peter Pan collar. Of course, she's got the tartan skirt and the Sperry Top-Siders. They're both collegiate stunners with their hair moussed to the heavens.

I must sigh or snort or something because simultaneously, they turn their heads from their private conversation to check me out—the lanky nobody slouched down in his seat, arms crossed over his track jacket, wearing anonymous gray sweatpants and a slacker's high tops. Still, my dad always says that a smile and a nod cost nothing, so I grin at these prepsters like we're old friends. I'm gratified when, taken aback, they quirk their mouths in annoyance and return to their self-absorbed cuddling and cooing.

I resume my watch on the hallway beyond the entrance.

Unofficially, this partitioned space in the student center, near the front entrance and beyond the newsstand, is known as the MTV room. Maybe once, other kids came to this only open television lounge on campus to watch the headlines or catch an episode of *Cheers*, but ever since the new music cable channel started broadcasting this last summer, the room's been a 24/7 assembly of New Wave zombies staring at the videos of Pat Benatar, Phil Collins, and Hall & Oates. I mean, I guess I'm among them, too, planted as I am in the front row, basking in the radiation of the cathode rays.

Mostly I'm keeping an eye on the foot traffic. There's a men's room twenty feet further down the hall that's the cruisiest tearoom on campus. Townies, staff, and students sidle into it all hours of the day, but the real bonus is that the student center building sits close to the touristy merchant's square adjacent. Often a curious, horny out-of-towner will make his way here, hunting for a willing mouth. And I'm more than willing. Anyone on the prowl will have to pass the lounge entrance to my right. I won't miss a one.

So far, there haven't been any passersby. Too early on a sleepy Saturday, or maybe I'm the only one with morning wood. In the meantime, I entertain myself with a little David Bowie. He's supposed to be bi, right? Whatever happened with that?

I might be in for a long haul this a.m. The only person roaming around is a custodian, his companion a bucket on wheels. I've slouched all the way down in my chair and am staring at the ceiling, listening to the music with my ears peeled, when someone says, "Wick." Startled, I peer into the hallway. No one. Then, "Wickham."

That's my name, all right. What can I say? My mom's a certified Jane Austen nut. It's only when I look the other direction, at the entrance from the student lounge, that I see the man standing there. He's lean and tall—as tall as I am, anyway. Older. Maybe fifty? He's bald with a fringe of gray hair orbiting the back of his head from one ear to the other. "Professor Poirier," I say, jumping to my feet.

The professor carries a battered leather briefcase in one hand and a cup of newsstand coffee in the other. He's wearing that whole higher education standard-issue uniform this morning. Tweed jacket, crisp blue button-down, tan slacks, leather belt, tasseled loafers. The guy's only concession to the weekend is an open collar and no tie. He takes me in, from dirty sneakers to tousled hair, then fixes me with a stare that unsettles my stomach and makes my dick harden. "Wick. I was wondering if we might take a walk and... discuss an assignment." His eyes flicker to the room's back corner.

His formality of speech is solely for the preppy couple beyond. They're paying no mind to us, though. I clear my throat and jog in the man's direction. "Certainly, professor," I say, playing the part of an eager, clean-cut student.

I follow several steps behind as he leads me from

the lounge, past the newsstand into the stairwell within the front entrance. Down we go into the student center's humid depths. Not a lot goes on down here. The cellar is where custodians store folding chairs and bleachers for special events and where lesser student organizations have their meeting rooms. Save for the echo of our soles slapping the tile, it's dead quiet.

I know exactly where we're going—to the basement men's room next to the student newspaper's offices. No one's working at the Flat Hat this early on a Saturday; its door is shut tight. I'd met Professor Poirier in this very tearoom a little over a year ago, my first day on campus. Hell, the first hour that I was on my own. After my folks had unloaded the car and seen my dorm room, we'd attended the President's Tea, then said our goodbyes. I'd immediately hared off to find the cruising spots.

Every campus has secret places where men gather to play. The library is usually a prime candidate, as are busier classroom buildings. But it was here in the Student Center, right across from Jefferson Hall, my old freshman dorm, within mere minutes, that I hit pay dirt.

The stall next to me had been occupied when I'd dropped my pants and sat down. Almost immediately, the leather shoe adjacent had slowly lifted and fallen, drawing closer. I'd responded in kind, matching him inch for inch until our feet touched. Then, following the man's beckoning finger, I'd left my stall for his and, for the first time, met Alvin Poirier, Professor of French and chair of the Modern Languages department.

Today, we skip all those preliminaries of man-to-man courtship. No dance of the Bass loafer and the cheap Converse. Men who know what they want don't need signals or signs. The minute we're beyond the shrieking men's room door, the professor abandons his cardboard cup on a sink, grabs me by the sleeve, then pulls me deeper within.

The tile-covered restroom is U-shaped, with wash stations opposite the door. Urinals and stalls sit on the other side of a wall. It's toward them that the older man tugs me around the bend, his echoing steps hastening toward our goal. Unlike the men's rooms directly above, the basement toilets have no outside windows; when my older buddy pulls me into the handicapped stall at the room's far end and latches its door, the gloom is perfect.

I'm a little breathless as I watch Professor Poirier set his briefcase next to the commode, then remove his jacket and fastidiously drape it on the door's hanger. He's not super handsome or anything, but the man excites me. Maybe I have a thing for authority figures. Whatever it is, I dig the way he makes me wait. I rest my butt on the metal grab bar while I watch him unbutton his shirt—just a single button more, enough to reveal a little chest hair—then release the clasp of his belt. Gravity drags his khakis to the floor. I reach out toward the goods, but he swats my hand away.

Finally, maybe even most importantly, with our eyes locked, he holds up his left hand and makes a show of unscrewing his wedding ring from the fourth finger. Yeah, I've always known the man is married. I've seen his wife. Hell, I've seen the whole family out and about. It's a super small town. All I care is that once the ring comes off, the Professor belongs to me.

"Jacket," he whispers, flicking his index finger in my direction. Without hesitation, I unzip and shimmy out of my red top. He folds the garment vertically into thirds, smooths it down, and drapes it carefully over the toilet's plumbing. "Shirt."

I'm wearing nothing beneath but a white Hanes tank top. I don't even hesitate. It's in his hands in a split second. He shakes the flimsy thing out and hangs it over my jacket. For a moment, he pauses. My dick stiffens as he regards my body. I know he likes it. I can tell by the glint in his eyes that I'm exactly what he hoped to find this morning.

I'm standing there, shivering not from the chill but anticipation, when he looks down. "Pants."

"Wha—?" Taking off my top is no biggie. I've done that for him before. But stripping all the way down is further than he's ever asked me to go, at least in a tearoom. "Really?" I jerk my head toward the hall. If anyone came in...campus security or something...

"Take off the pants, Wick." I want the man so badly that I'll do anything he asks, but self-preservation makes me hesitate. Then, in one swift and unexpected motion, he yanks down my sweats, tangling them around my knees. If I'd gone commando this morning, like I usually do when cruising, my dick would've popped up and out on release. I'm wearing a jock, though—so all that happens is the head busts out the pouch's side. Not as impressive. But it still makes a statement, I guess. "All the way."

In for a penny, in for a pound. I stretch the elasticized ankles around my shoes and, with some maneuvering, manage to remove the offending garment.

"You're my favorite boy." The Professor's voice is no more than a murmur as he shakes out the fleece, folds the sweats in half, and rests them atop my other clothing. "You know that, right?"

He probably says this to every undergrad hungry for him, but in this moment, standing in that toilet stall wearing nothing more than a jock and a pair of beat-up high tops, I'm willing to believe every word. My dick nudges out another inch as he moves in. His warm hands travel from my armpits to my waist as he pulls me close.

"Yes, sir," I breathe, completely under his spell. In the wake of his touch, gooseflesh blooms. My breath rasps as his lips press gently on my shoulder, my collarbone, the spot where neck meets jaw.

"And you know what I most want from my favorite boy, don't you?"

"I do, sir."

He seizes my upper arms and pulls me in for a kiss. I've taken these walks with Professor Poirier dozens of times. Sometimes here, sometimes to his office, usually just to the nearest available men's room. Every damn time, he reduces me to a quivering, compliant mess. He's not the most handsome fellow out there. The guy's old enough to be my dad. Maybe even older. But every time I come across the professor on campus and catch him staring at me, I can see the certainty in his eyes. He knows, just knows, that in a matter of minutes, he can have me stripped down and begging for him.

That kind of confidence really turns me on.

"You want a good grade from me, don't you, Wick?" Both of us are around six-three, but in his strong grasp, I feel like a wee little rag doll. "You want that easy A, right?"

"Yes, sir," I say, my head lolling weakly. I'm not in any of the Professor's courses. Never needed French. Never will. If he wants to make believe I'm earning some extra credit, though, I'm all in on the fantasy.

He's pushing me down now. My sneakers squeal on the dirty floor; my knees collide with the cold tile.

Hands on my shoulders, he keeps me at arm's length. What I desire still hides behind crisp blue cotton. "Don't have to be smart when you're pretty. Isn't that right, Wick?"

"No, sir. I mean, yes, sir." My prize is so close. I can feel the heat from his groin.

The Professor laughs at my confusion. "Exactly what I'm saying." He tips my head up so that I'm looking into his eyes once more. "A boy doesn't have to be a scholar when he's lanky and blond..." He runs fingers through my hair, which immediately flops over my forehead and into my eyes once more. "...and pretty. And a good...little...cocksucker."

I gasp at the last word. Don't get me wrong. I've heard it plenty. Yet when Professor Poirier says it, he switches off what's left of my thinking brain. My dick strains in the jock, craving release. A stupid hole is exactly what I need to be.

Now that I'm kneeling before him, the Professor reaches for the band of his plaid boxers. I'm already drooling in anticipation of what's to follow. "You ready to suck my cock...cocksucker?" This man knows how to play me like a fiddle. I intend to verbalize my assent, but it comes out as a grunt, feral and hungry. He gets my message. Slowly, deliberately, he pulls down his shorts.

And there it is. Out leaps what I've wanted all along, the huge and heavy prize for which I've thirsted, the very source of all the man's swagger. Listen, I'm a big enough boy. Bigger than most, at about seven and three-quarter inches, maybe eight when I'm arching my back or especially turned on. Professor Poirier, though, is the proud owner of a nine-and-a-half-inch slab of man meat that is both the hardest and thickest thing I've ever seen. If I were hauling around that mighty log, I'd have confidence to spare, too. The man is the very definition of the word *cocksure*.

More heat emanates from the monster as I dive for it. No longer do I care about my near nakedness in a public restroom. I don't mind the discomfort of kneecaps grinding on tile. All I want is that dick, that massive plank jutting out at eye level. And I want it down my throat. Immediately.

Professor Poirier collapses in upon himself and gasps as I devour him. He must be relishing the sight of a stripped-down student crazy for him and his tool. I know he loves my mouth; he's told me so many times in the past. I don't need to hear the words. Those sighs cascading from his lips, the tightening skin of his scrotum, the jets of his precum that paint my gums and palate—I can read all these signs clearly as any textbook.

For long minutes, I slobber my way up and down that beautiful dick, barely conscious of anything other than my hunger. Only when he pulls me off and leans down for a kiss do I realize how loud I've been in my unbridled lust; the sounds of my snarls and slavering still echo throughout the restroom. His tongue invades my mouth, forceful and deep. He must taste himself in there. Then he releases me and grabs hold of the partition top while I return to work.

This sensation of stretched lips against concrete shaft intoxicates me. I don't even know how long I worship at his altar, trying to engulf as much of that monster as I can. He knows I'll suck for as long as he needs, but selfishness urges me to initiate what usually finishes him off—one hand clamped firmly at the base of his cock, with the other stroking his balls. Even as my fingertips tickle his sac, I feel globs of salty goo oozing from his tip.

"No hands," he proclaims. His fingers sting when they slap away my wrists. For a minute or two, I obey. Well, I try. Honestly, I try. But I am so much in love with this dick and the way that it abuses the recesses of my throat that I can't help myself. I curl one fist at the base and let the other encircle his nuts. He sighs again, this time with exasperation. "I said, no hands."

I'm too far gone, though, to heed the note of warning in his voice. I'm in a cock frenzy, powered by a deep need to make the man shoot. It's only when I'm shoved back against the stall door and deprived of that beautiful dick that I come to my senses. But it's too late: he's seized both my forearms and somehow trussed them together. I feel my arms yanked up and sideways. My vision clears, and I understand what's happened. The Professor has jerked the leather belt from his trousers, threaded it through the buckle, and pulled tight the noose in a sort of lasso to restrain my hands at the wrist. I watch in disbelief—and then excitement—as he knots the pointed end of the belt to the handicapped grab bar on the wall.

Oh. Fuck.

"When I say no hands," he snarls, testing to make sure I'm secured, "I mean, *no hands*. You understand?"

I, too, tug at my makeshift shackle. I could probably wriggle out of it with some effort, but I don't care to. Gratitude shines in my eyes. "Yeah. I mean, yes, sir."

That's when he grabs the back of my head and shoves his dick down my throat. I've got knees sprawled in one direction, neck pulled in another, bound hands twisting me in a third, and none of it is comfortable. But I don't care. I just want him to keep skull fucking me. I'm his cocksucker. It's what I was made for.

I've lost track of time again when, suddenly, he stops. His palms have been pressing hard against my ears. They'll be red and painful for hours. Totally worth it. It's not until I look up and see the professor pressing an index finger against his lips that I realize something's happened: the sound of footsteps and running water on the other side of the wall, in the sink area. Replaying the last half-minute in my cock-fogged brain, I can even remember hearing the restroom door's metallic screech as someone opened it. I'd been too far gone to heed.

There's not a lot I can do about my clothing situation in my manacled state, but I can keep still and quiet. Silence is the first form of self-preservation every cruiser learns. The professor makes no move to untie me. In fact, he seems to be getting a kick out of having a naked, shackled sophomore at his feet in a toilet stall while a stranger washes his hands around the corner. Still gesturing to keep quiet, he gyrates forward with his hips, first grazing my lips with his sticky cock head, then sliding between them.

I don't have much choice but to comply. I gaze up at the professor with adoration. Right now, he is the hottest man in the world. I'm content to be stripped down and on the edge of discovery, so long as he keeps sliding the length of his shaft in and out of my mouth with a slow, slow rhythm. I'm more alert now, though; I keep an ear out as I hear the stranger turn off the taps, pull out paper towels, toss them into the bin. There are footsteps that sound like they might be coming our way. Then, only a second or two before I can panic, I hear them turn and walk back. The men's room door loudly opens and closes. Then silence.

"Open up, cocksucker," the Professor whispers. Once more, he seizes my head and forces it down on his meat. There's no way I intend to back down from this silent challenge. I'll keep up with every thrust of his battering ram as he pounds it into me.

It's with a muffled roar that finally he comes. The sound is dampened by his hands on my ears again and by my own sobbing and choking as I gulp for air. I taste a flood of seed on my tongue, then another; he pulls out and allows the next couple of jets to land on my face and chest. My eyes are wet and teary from the use I've endured. My nose is dripping. Runnels of drool cascade down my chin to mix with his cum. I'm a fucking mess, but I still look up to him with supplication as he wipes the last drip of semen onto my cheek.

I can breathe again. It's difficult, but I rasp in a lungful of cool air. His belt buckle bites against my wrist bone, but it's his call when I should be set free. Only when he stoops down to reach for my red and dripping cock, which by now has totally escaped the mesh pouch, do I try to close my knees and shy away. "You don't want to shoot?"

Shooting is what I want more than anything, in this moment. There'll be hell to pay with M.J. if I do, though. "I've got a date later," I tell him.

He nods and chuckles a bit. When I say stuff like that, I always get the impression that I amuse him. "I think you might have another date right now," he tells me, nodding in the direction over my shoulder.

What the fuck? When did he open the stall door? A stranger stands outside. Some townie or tourist, I'm guessing, by the fancy Members Only jacket and suede moccasins. He's maybe in his late thirties, dark-haired, and sports a Freddie Mercury mustache. His

501s are unbuttoned so he can stroke a fat six inches. It's probably that guy we heard washing his hands earlier. And he's been watching us for—well, I don't know how long.

"You're going to be a good boy, aren't you, Wick?" asks the Professor as he returns his wedding band to his ring finger. "Earn a little extra credit while I supervise?"

"Yes, sir," I whisper, as I strain as close to the stranger as the professor's belt will allow. My mouth opens wide.

Go to my alma mater, my dad had told me back in high school. *You won't lack for a social life there.*

He wasn't lying.

2

TAKE HOME ASSIGNMENT

This is how all my dates with M.J. begin: in the front seat of his '76 Chevette with his hand shoved down the front of my pants. It's not as erotic as it sounds. In fact, it's outright painful. "Christ," I protest, squirming out of his clutch when he squeezes so hard that bolts of sheer pain shoot from my nuts to my elbows. "That's enough. I didn't jack off, okay?"

The tourist parking lot where I've climbed into his car is a pretty public place to maul my balls. He's incredibly weird about being seen with me. Yet M.J.'s grizzly beard is practically lying on my belly, and his forearm thrusts halfway down the gray fleece sweatpants I've been wearing since the morning. I don't get it.

"Satisfied?" I snarl. I hate being subjected to his testicular examination before he'll consent to take me home.

"Nice and firm," he decrees, finally withdrawing. He shakes out his fingers, then raises them to his nostrils and takes a sniff. It's not as gross as it sounds. I'd taken a shower after my early morning antics.

All right, it might be a little gross.

"Whatever." I buckle up and slide down in the seat, ignoring him as he turns the ignition and pulls out across the gravel.

We're a quarter of a mile from our rendezvous point before he notices my sulk. "Come on. Is it a crime I like you ready to go?"

I refrain from pointing out that I'm just about always ready to go. "It's fucking humiliating, is all," I mumble through my fist.

"You know I don't like that word." He sniffs prissily like he's considering washing my mouth out in soap. "It's so Anglo-Saxon."

See, M.J. hates it when I masturbate before we meet. He's issued standing orders not to touch myself for twenty-four hours before a date. He has a notion that he can tell by the density of my balls if I've shot a load. If they're hard and firm like—I don't know—walnuts or something, I've been a good boy. If they're the least bit spongy, he assumes I've been shaking hands with the milkman.

It's stupid. The one time I lied, though, he'd given the jewels a squeeze, called me out on it, and kicked me from the car. Lately, I've just kept my hands off the thing before we meet.

The agreement doesn't say I can't spend my morning chugging strange dick, though. I love a good loophole.

M.J. lives in a condo complex out on the heavily wooded edge of town. The shade's so deep that even now, around noon, it feels like twilight. We have a standard routine on arrival. I wait in the Chevette's passenger seat until he's scurried inside. Then, when the coast is clear, and he's given the signal, I crouch low and scamper up the walk and through the front door. Once I'm in, M.J. locks the door and fastens the chain. I've never seen any neighbors, so the cloak-and-dagger bullshit seems like overkill.

But I should've recognized the man's paranoia from the start. Two months ago, I'd met M.J. in the second-cruisiest tearoom on campus, on the second floor of the library. Nights, when I'm supposed to be studying, I'll sometimes set myself up at a carrel near the restroom door to keep an eye on who's going in or out. If someone interesting catches my eye, I can scoop my books into my bag and be in the heat of the action in half a minute.

The evening I met M.J., I'd already given a couple of hand jobs to anonymous dicks beneath the marble stall partition. Then the tearoom door creaked open, and a man in his mid-forties strode to the urinal opposite. Through the crack of the stall door, I checked him out: a beard to his sternum, dark-haired, bespectacled, wearing the same tweed-jacket-and-khakis ensemble of all the male professors.

He'd looked over his shoulder. I'd stared back through the crack. Once he'd caught my stare and we were sure of each other, I opened my stall to show him that I was rock-hard and stroking, jeans around my ankles. With an eye on the door, he stepped over to present five inches protruding from his unzipped khakis. I opened wide and sucked him through his fly as he ran his fingers through my hair. The guy shot a sour load on my tongue within seconds, then lingered in my wet mouth until he'd softened again.

Zipping up, he'd bent down to whisper in my ear. "Count to three hundred, then meet me outside the front."

I'd barely had time to process the bizarre instructions before he'd disappeared from the tearoom. I've done weirder things for uglier guys, though, so I busied myself cleaning up while I ticked off the numbers, then made my way downstairs and outside.

My bearded trick darted out of the shadows where he'd been waiting to murmur something else. "Follow me—but stay twenty feet back."

He was off like a shot, looking both ways to make sure no one watched, walking so quickly I had to jog to keep up. He'd led me on a merry chase across the greater part of the north campus until he'd ducked into the building that housed the Economics Department. I lost him on the second floor; he'd had to grab and pull me into his office as I wandered by.

Once the door was closed, he'd pushed me up against the wall and growled in my ear, "You know what you're doing with those lips, boy."

"I like to suck," I'd said in a low voice to match his. "Love getting fucked, too."

"I don't like Anglo-Saxon language," he'd warned for the first—but not last—time. But he'd looked me up and down with speculation. "I want to take you out for a meal. Saturday. Then I'll take you home. You'll come." Honestly, I was convinced he wanted more of my lips right then and there, but no. Already, he'd opened the office door to hustle me out. "You'll get more of what you want, then." Then he'd closed the door in my face.

That's how I first met Madison Jefferson Franklin Washington, a.k.a. M.J. I thought being named Wickham was bad. It's a far cry better than having your birth certificate clobbered by the U.S. Constitution. The question lingered, though, as I stumbled back to my dorm: I'd gone through all that espionage nonsense for so little?

It's a question I always ask when we're alone, like now. "Get naked for me," he commands once I'm in the condo foyer. Unlike Professor Poirier, M.J. doesn't fold my clothes; he'd probably consign my sloppy athletic wear to the incinerator if he thought he could get away with the deed. I kick off my shoes, strip off the rest of my gear, and follow him up to the bedroom. He's already flat on his back atop the mattress, trousers pulled to mid-thigh. "I know you want this," he says, brandishing his tool.

I like sucking dick, but I won't perjure myself. I crawl, panther-like, between his hairy legs, grab his cock at the base, then wrap my lips around it.

"Suck it, boy." M.J.'s eyes are closed. He's lost in whatever fantasy is playing out in his imagination. "Suck me good."

M.J.'s dick has a big old mole on its top—a flat, squishy button about an inch and a half from the base. Every time I go down on him, I cringe to think of accidentally raking my teeth across the thing. I always make sure to hook my index finger over it as an indication of where I can safely bottom out. Having to hold back makes me grumpy, though. I miss a good sore back-of-the-throat feeling I can savor for a couple of hours after.

But I get the job done. When M.J. finally squirts out a teaspoon of fluid, I make a show of swallowing loudly and showing appreciation with a grunt.

I roll on my back and give him a minute to recuperate. There'll be another round of the same old same old, after a meal. Eventually, he rolls over and gives me an avuncular peck on the lips. "You smell like semen. Go rinse your mouth."

"It's *your* fucking semen," I point out as I stomp away from the bed.

"Anglo-Saxon. And hurry back. I've got something for you."

Why do I keep seeing M.J.? Valid question. I often ask it myself. Partly, it's because his secrecy and attempts at subterfuge amuse me. It's also that I, like most kids on campus, don't have a car of my own. Sometimes I just want to get the hell away from the campus, with its frats and jocks and constant reminders I should be studying.

A lot of it, though, has to do with the presents. There's always a box from one of the better clothing stores in town waiting for me after I perform. Once, it was a watch, hideous and heavy; another time, a new leather billfold with a twenty-dollar bill tucked inside because M.J. says it's bad luck to gift an empty wallet. Between rounds of genteel oral, M.J. will drive me out along the river, across the ferry, or on some other dull excursion. Mid-afternoon, during a lull between the lunch and dinner crowds, we'll end up at Nick's Seafood Pavilion, all the way out in Yorktown, where he'll treat me to whatever I want off the menu. Even dessert.

It's the closest I've ever come in my life to actual dating. If it means I have to put up with some bland sex and a mole on the dick...who's it hurting?

"Surprise!" he says, beaming when I return from a bout with his bottle of Listerine. In my absence, he's laid out several boxes from the merchant's square. The man's so excited at his generosity that he denies me the pleasure of opening them myself. There's a sweater of some sort, a dress shirt, a pair of dress pants...even shoes, argyle socks, and a belt from the leather goods store.

Remember those scenes in Cinderella when cartoon fauna dresses the heroine while she twirls around and sings? Well, the next few minutes are exactly like that, except instead of flocks of bluebirds and squirrels, I get one hairy bearded econ professor stuffing me into my new outfit. And no singing. Five minutes later, M.J. runs a wet comb through my hair, parts it on the side where no part has ever naturally fallen, and slicks it across the top of my head.

I blink without recognition at the figure in the full-length mirror on his closet door. M.J. lays his hand on my shoulder and admires his handiwork. "Don't you look handsome!"

No. No, sir. I do not. What I look like is a kid dressed up for the Young Republicans campus recruitment drive. In a goddamned sweater vest, no less. What has he done to my hair? I pat at it, unconvinced it can stay tamed for long.

He mistakes doubt for admiration. "Come on," he urges. "I've got a whole afternoon planned."

M.J.'s agenda, it turns out, involves touring a historic plantation a dozen miles away. They're a dime a dozen in this section of the South. Maybe certain images come to mind when envisioning an old Virginia estate: a genteel country mansion with Palladian columns and classical proportions, facade whitewashed and gleaming, its verandah covered with bougainvillea. Forget that. This plantation isn't one of the popular tourist spots, probably because it's a two-room shanty on a rolling bank of weeds located along a particularly smelly turn of the river. A dispirited woman hands out a slip of paper (free) printed with the house's history and sells souvenirs (overpriced) on the shack's front porch.

Touring the place doesn't take that long. We're the only ones here, so M.J. doesn't even make me walk at a distance. In fact, when we brave the stink and stroll along the river in the shade of the wild sumacs, he's emboldened to give my shoulders a quick squeeze.

Though my feet ache in the shiny brown loafers that he's gifted me, and though I'm sweltering in the checkered sweater vest, the feeling is kind of...well, it feels kind of nice when someone does something for you. Even in a half-assed way. Then M.J. gets some burrs on his khakis and starts raising a fuss, and the feeling disappears.

It's when we're well away from the plantation, but still on the dirt country road leading back to civilization, that everything goes wrong. The Chevette shudders with a terrible grinding noise that's halfway between an amplified dentist's drill and a banshee's scream. It's the worst thing I've ever heard, yet M.J. seems determined to ignore it. The vibrations get so bad, though, that I start worrying about a nosebleed—or worse, an explosion.

"You've got to stop the car," I tell him, clutching the dashboard. The screeching triples in volume when he attempts steering around a bend. He can barely maneuver the wheel. I have to yell, *"Stop the car!"* at the top of my voice to be heard. Then I tumble out the door and glare at him as he emerges sheepishly from the driver's side.

"It doesn't sound that bad to me," he blusters. It's difficult to hear, though, over the ringing in my ears. "Get back in."

"No way."

He looks around wildly, still paranoid that out here in the middle of nowhere, someone might see us. "Get back in the car."

I shake my head.

"What do you want me to do?" M.J. throws his arms in the air and shouts. "Call a tow truck? Go to some stranger's house and phone Triple A? Over a little noise? Okay, a big noise. But...what're they going to say about us?" He's almost hysterical at the thought of being seen with me. Which makes me feel fantastic, of course. "Who am I going to tell them you are?!"

I can't believe what I'm hearing. My dad always says—yeah, he's never short on opinions—that unless someone's writing your checks, you don't owe them explanations. Some stuff is nobody's business. It's a philosophy that works for me. While M.J. whips himself into a purple-faced tizzy, I turn my back and stomp off down the road. Someone has to do what needs doing.

The nearest farmhouse sits a good half-mile away. The couple inside are super friendly when I explain my car's broken down. The man calls a nearby tow service he knows, and while I wait, the woman pours some sweet iced tea and packs a sympathy bag of Fig Newtons. From a distance, on the walk back, I can see that neither M.J. nor the Chevette are going anywhere. So, I take my sweet time. The tow truck is just pulling up by the time I rejoin M.J.

The driver who heaves himself out of his cab looks almost exactly like Yukon Cornelius, that enormous, red-headed, bearded guy from the Rudolph Christmas special. "Folks," he says in a broad Southern drawl. He looks me up and down, then at M.J., who's avoiding eye contact, and back at me again. "Don't y'all worry," he assures us when I step forward. "I'll get you and your dad where you need to be."

M.J. chokes, off to the side, but I understand the driver's assumption. This uncomfortable new outfit makes me look like an M.J. Junior, I realize. Hilarious. "My dad and I appreciate that," I tell the man, sounding super friendly. "Dad thinks it's nothing, but I'm pretty sure the axle's screwed."

"Don't want to be driving on a damaged axle," says

the man as he tugs on a big pair of leather work gloves. "Should listen to your son."

"Yeah," I say, grinning like a madman. I punch M.J. on the shoulder. "You should listen to your son." M.J. fumes while I relish the moment—and the Fig Newtons, which I pointedly keep to myself.

In the driver's front seat, on the way back to town, the driver and I keep up a stream of chatter. "You and your dad were out looking at the plantation, I'm guessing?"

I'm wedged in the middle between Yukon Cornelius and M.J., arms crossed to keep my elbows out of the way. Ignoring the professor's aggrieved sigh, I reply, "We sure were. Dad wasn't having fun, but I really get into old stuff." I look M.J. dead in the face, though he avoids me. "The older the better."

"Real nice of him to go, then. It's great when a dad and son do things together."

"We do a lot together," I assure him. Then I attempt something daring, just because after all the afternoon's stress, I'm feeling ornery. With my arms still crossed, my left fingers reach out and tweak M.J.'s nipple. I can feel him jump about three feet out of his seat, but the driver doesn't notice. "Fun things."

If M.J. could've slapped away my hand, he would've. But Yukon Cornelius can't see. As I continue to squeeze my so-called dad's nipple and run my knuckles up and down his rib cage, M.J. begins to relax. By the time we're nearly back to his place, he's even unwound enough to allow his fingertips to rub and bob against my own.

It's when we're back in the condo parking lot, waving at the truck driver as he pulls out to drop off the Chevette at the garage, that M.J. turns to me and speaks for the first time since our argument. "Thank you."

I shrug.

"You handled that all by yourself. It's not even your car."

I shrug again.

"You're right. Maybe I overthink situations."

At least his apology is hitting the correct notes. "It's all right." Then I add, "Dad," because I can't resist one more jibe.

"Hey," he says. "Son?"

"What?"

That's when he leans in close. His voice is a growl. "I have never wanted to fuck you senseless more than I do right now."

I swallow hard. My mouth opens to declare he's being Anglo-Saxon. Know what's better than being a smart ass, though? Being smart enough to shut up and get that ass fucked. The two of us stare each other down and, as if on cue, run inside the condo.

Clothes fly everywhere. That damned sweater vest is the first to go, followed by the penny loafers. This may be the first time I've seen M.J. fully naked; he's a beast. Fur covers his chest and back. There's even a thick pelt on his shoulders that stretches to his knuckles like a stole. "Wow," I say, appraising his body. "You're hairy, Dad."

It's this one word that's driving him wild. In the truck, I figured it was a blow to his dignity, but no, it's a straight-up aphrodisiac, a hit of poppers under the nostrils. Just hearing me say it makes his dick stiffen and leap. His eyes glint like obsidian. "Keep calling me that, son. See what happens."

"Yeah, Dad? You want me to keep calling you *Dad*, Dad?" I stalk over to the bed, flop down on my back, and stretch like a cat waking from a nap. "What happens if I do...dad?"

He's frozen in place, staring. Then he leaps. I've never seen the man move so quickly. My back drags the sheets askew as he propels me across them. When my skull collides with the headboard, I don't complain. I can't. His lips completely cover mine; his beard grinds against my smooth skin as his tongue delves deep. "What happens when a boy says that," he aspirates, over the sounds of the bedside drawer sliding open, then closed, "is that the boy gets his ass fucked." With a mighty wallop, his open hand smacks my butt. I yelp with pleasure and savor the warmth that spreads from the point of impact.

Yeah, I've never been into M.J. as much as I am right now. I feel a glob of something cold and slippery against my hole—petroleum jelly, by the smell. I lift my legs and hook my arms around my knees to open myself as wide as possible. "Fuck me, Dad," I beg. Sincerity makes me moan. "I need my dad's big dick inside me."

"You little slut. My boy's a whore for Dad's fat dong." His body is positioned between my thighs now. He's applying more of the Vaseline to his cock. As I've said, it's not a big dick, so I doubt it'll cause much of a—

"Fuck, Dad!" My shout fills the little bedroom when his mushroom head pops through the outmost ring. He should've been doing this to me all along instead of those almost chaste blow jobs. The man feels amazing, sliding inside. He's filling a void I never knew was there. "Oh, thank you," I say, clutching at him as he hits the base. "Thank you, thank you, sir." It hurts some, but that ache is what I need right now.

"Damn, boy," he growls, pushing in a little more deeply just to show me who's boss. "You feel so good."

"You make it good." I shake my head in disbelief. M.J. knows what he's doing. "Please fuck me, Dad."

Every time I use that word, his dick throbs and swells. Damn, I wish I'd known about his kink months ago. "Yeah, I'll fuck you, slut. Gonna knock up that boy hole, Son."

"Do it," I beg.

He lifts my hips clear off the bed in his frenzy to sink in more deeply. He doesn't hold back. Within a couple of minutes, he's sliding all the way out, then driving back in. My fingertips search for his nipples and discover diamond hard points beneath the dense fur. Twisting and pinching them makes him fuck harder, so I dig in. "You're going to make me blast my load, boy," he warns.

"I need it, sir," I plead. He's grasping the top of the headboard, ankle-deep in bedclothes. By now, my ass is high in the air; I'm basically doing a shoulder stand while M.J. towers above me, jackhammering my hole. The bedroom echoes with his grunts and the sticky sounds of our mating. I urge him on. "Spunk me up, Dad. You made that hole. Fucking flood it."

"Oh, fuck," he says. The Anglo-Saxonisms are flying now. "Fuuuuuck. Gonna blow! Gonna pop off deep in my boy."

"Do it!"

"You ready?"

Am I ever! Usually, when M.J. shoots, it's almost completely silent, save for a little huff at the end. Now, though, he's letting out a bellow straight from the diaphragm that starts low both in volume and pitch, then gets louder and higher until it erupts in a choked howl. His cock contracts and expands; I feel the warmth when his balls release.

We remain frozen in place for what feels like a good minute. At last, his breathing subsides, and I feel him withdraw. There's a gush of wetness on my balls and down my crack. Then, as M.J. steps off the bed, my hips crash down to bounce on the mattress.

"Gotta clean up," he says. "Then you should go."

I guess the moment is over. My dick still wants attention, and my hole is still hungry, but clearly, M.J.'s fire has been doused. The excitement of a moment ago only sets into sharper relief my usual post-sex disappointment with the man. I retreat under the covers.

"Go? How?" I point out. "It's dark. You're seriously going to make me walk four miles back to campus? Through the woods?"

"Sleep over, then," he calls from the bathroom. I hear the sounds of the taps, then the shower starts. "I don't care." Just the thing a guy wants to hear from his date, right? "We'll figure it out in the morning."

He's right about one thing: I'm stuck here. That part's fine. My night owl roommate won't notice or care. We already have a detente established: I leave him undisturbed to sleep until two in the afternoon if he refrains from blasting his Rush albums after midnight. But I'm starved. We never made it to Nick's after the plantation.

I make a nest among the sheets and coverlets while I listen to the sounds of M.J. scrubbing any trace of me from his skin. At least I'd enjoyed that nice lady's Fig Newtons, though a plastic baggie of cookies does not a dinner make. It was going to be a long, hungry night.

Still, I guess the combination of all that day's sex, stress, and exercise took its toll. Because next thing I

know, I'm blinking my eyes at sunlight seeping between the slats of the drawn shades. It's morning. The
water's still running. Or I guess, given that it's hours
later, it's running a second time. M.J. must have gotten
up early for another shower because the bed is empty.
Ignoring my morning wood, I roll over to face the
door.

A boy stands by the bed, dressed in a hoodie,
jeans, and sneakers. A boy with hair the color of a new
penny and the widest, greenest eyes I've ever seen. I
guess he's my age—or even a year or two older. He's
got his hands in his pockets and his head tilts to the
side as he regards me with birdlike curiosity. "Who—
who are you?" I stammer in astonishment.

His voice is equally as quiet. "I'm David," is his
baritone reply. "And who are you?"

3

CAMPUS GREEK LIFE

I'm not at my best, mornings. That's why, upon seeing a strange kid standing at the bedside, I rub my eyes and blink in case I'm dreaming. But nope, he's still there, motionless, staring, not seeming to notice how confused I am.

Maybe I should get the hell away. This David guy could be M.J.'s boyfriend, for all I know. Perhaps he's not happy about finding some strange dude in his lover's bed. He doesn't seem hostile, though. When our eyes meet, his lips almost twitch into a smile. "What are you doing here?" I ask.

He shrugs. That's it. That's all I get. It's like he heard all my dad's talks about not owing anyone explanations. "You didn't tell me your name."

"Wick," I say. Then, to fill the silence, I elaborate, "Wickham."

"Wick," he repeats. When he steps forward and reaches in my direction, my first reflex is to retreat. All he does, though, is pinch the duvet by the corner. Those eyes, green as apples on the stem, meet mine once more. He tilts his head and raises his eyebrows, asking an unspoken question. I relinquish my hold and allow him to draw back the coverings in equally silent consent.

My body lies before him. I shiver, feeling naked. Not merely unclothed—utterly and completely exposed. I wonder what I must look like to him. A skinny kid, barely making any progress in bulking up. A crazy amount of blond fur on my legs, none on my chest. Even crazier hair. M.J.'s attempts yesterday to tamp it down only made it angry, so now it's a wild tsunami rising from my scalp. I lie there, unmoving, as his eyes flick from nipple to nipple, down the repeated ridges and valleys of ribs beneath my skin. Then to my navel. An outie, much to my regret. But he doesn't linger long there.

When David's eyes reach my morning wood, his front teeth scrape his bottom lip. The softest fricative tumbles forth and evaporates in the morning sunlight. Seeing his big eyes widen makes my dick jump. I can't help it. I'm attracted to him in a way I never am for guys my age. Older men are my thing. Bossy types who know what they want and expect me to provide it. Hell, I've made a career of fucking my way through the faculty here. David is so pretty, though. Like so many redheads, his skin is pale and translucent. With a bonus of candy-colored eyes and hair like spun copper, he looks as fragile as a child's doll—yet somehow, he's essentially masculine, lean, and solid. Definitely not a preppie.

Perhaps he's thinking something similar about me because after David replaces the duvet with care as if he's tucking me in, his fingers riff through my hair. His knuckles stroke the side of my face. "Meet me later," he says in a whisper.

I'm confused. Didn't I just meet him a moment ago? "Whuh?"

In the bathroom, the shower shuts off. David glances over his shoulder. When he speaks again, his voice is urgent. "You know the amphitheater? By the lake? Behind the campus?"

I nod. For decades, during the summers, the amphitheater had hosted a production called *Revolutionary Glory*, a patriotic pageant for the tourists lauding the colonial days. It was full of speeches, flag waving, and canned fife and drum cues but had closed down for good about five years ago. I'd seen the thing on its last legs sometime during middle school, with a bunch of disinterested actors stomping around in moth-eaten pilgrim costumes, declaiming at the tops of their lungs. Good riddance.

"Meet me behind it, in the dirt lot. Five o'clock."

I nod again, before I really know to what I'm agreeing. Meet him in a parking lot? Why?

"Promise."

"Okay, okay. I promise." Already, though, I'm regretful. I don't know this kid, after all.

He takes a step back and crosses his arms as M.J. pads into the room, still steaming from the shower. The professor seems unsurprised at the sight of the redhead in his bedroom. "You're early," is all he says before unhooking the towel from his waist and using it to dry the mostly nonexistent hair on his head.

David doesn't seem taken aback by the professor's nudity. He gazes down at the floor, though, while M.J. towels off. "I remembered where you leave your spare key."

Hell, I've no idea where M.J. keeps his spare key. I didn't know he had one. It's obvious this other boy is my predecessor in the man's bed. How long ago and how long it lasted, I've no idea.

"I guess you two met," says M.J., slipping on some

white briefs and black socks. "David's got his own truck. I thought you could drop off Wick on campus; then we'll head to the garage. Then you'll bring me back home, depending on how long the repairs will take. Right?" David inclines his head in agreement, not really seeming to mind having his Sunday morning plans made for him. His eyes slide my way, though, as I crawl out from beneath the duvet and plant my feet on the floor. "All right. Chop-chop. Get your things."

My eyes meet David's. Once again, his lips conceal the slightest of smiles. "I'll start the truck," he murmurs, and disappears.

The ride back to campus in David's beat-up blue Ford pickup is awkward. So awkward. Once again, I find myself stuck in the middle, but this time with a pile of gift boxes on my lap. There's no way M.J. intends to allow me to escape without yesterday's presents, which he's collected and re-packed. I feel like some kind of kept boy, sneaking back to the dorm with the undeniable proof of my gold-digging. M.J. keeps up a monologue all the way back; he and David share enough private jokes and history that I feel like an outsider. I pick up that David's a senior and an English major, but otherwise, he's not much of a talker.

When David pulls into the tourist parking lot, a few blocks from the foot of the campus, I realize I'm not the only one used to accommodating M.J.'s paranoia. He stops in practically the same space from which M.J. and I had departed, yesterday. "It was fun, kiddo," the professor says. He opens the passenger door and slides out to let me free. "Not sure when we can do it again. A lot depends on when I get the Chevette back, I guess, and…"

He's still rambling as I struggle across the padded

bench with my armful of gift boxes. That's when I feel David's hand on my wrist, then the warmth of his chin near my ear. "Five o'clock," he whispers. "Please come."

The boy doesn't look my way again—not when I turn to thank him, though I'm not given much of a chance since M.J. is already shoving his way back inside. Not when they back out. Not even when they crawl by, on the way to the exit, gravel popping and sputtering beneath the truck's tires.

I'd really craved a last glance from David, too.

And I'm torn. Part of me aches, in a new and unfamiliar way, to meet this other kid again. To find out what makes him tick. Why does he want to see me, of all people? A boy that pretty could have any man he wanted. Surely, he wouldn't settle for a scrawny sleazester like me.

Then there's this rule I have about not fucking around with other students. Okay, I break it all the time. There's that frat boy I met in the Tucker Hall men's room when he caught my eye. For a while, I had an on-again, off-again fling with a transfer student living in the Spanish House. And I don't know how many of those dicks I've jerked off understall in the library belong to other kids my age.

Okay, it's not so much a hard and fast rule as a guideline I feel free to ignore when my dick is hard.

The tourists and townies I pick up in the tearooms, I'm unlikely to see again. The faculty knows how to keep things discreet. I've always regarded other students as a risk. They aren't as savvy, for one thing. This isn't a big city where guys like me can be what they want to be. This is a Southern backwater where nobody's going to blink when some freak gets the beating he deserves. Hanging around with the wrong sort can't lead to anything good. That's why I never get myself into any situations where I can't pull up my sweats and run for it.

Those eyes, though...

That's why I find myself trudging up the road to the old amphitheater at the very back of the campus, with the minute hand rounding on five. Honestly, I spend most of the walk convinced I'm going to be punked, but once I round the thicket of wild sumacs separating the drive from the road, I spy David sitting on the bed of his truck. His legs kick the air as he waits. At the sound of my sneakers trudging across the dirt and wet leaves, he hops down, closes his gate, and wipes off his hands.

He's still wearing the hoodie and jeans from the morning, though he's added a denim jacket and raised his hood now that it's cooler. A fringe of red hair peeks out beneath the fleece. "You came," he says in a soft voice.

He looks so serious—but I'm no better. I can scarcely look him in the eye. "Yeah," I say. "So..."

"Come on." He's already walking at a fast pace. I scramble to catch up. No one comes out this way any-more, save the occasional canoeist heading down to the lake. The outdoor theater hasn't seen a crowd since the Bicentennial. Layer upon layer of leaves and pine needles form a spongy mattress underfoot that makes keeping pace with David a challenge.

He seems to have a destination in mind. He leads me through the trees, then down a hill in the direction of the water. Every step of the way, I'm trying to figure out exactly where we might be heading. I mean, I've done stuff in the woods before, but it's not ideal. "Gotta be careful of poison oak out here, I bet." All he does is turn, grace me with another of those half-smiles, and walk on.

I keep following, just to be with him.

It's not until we veer off the hill and in the direction of a large cinderblock construction in the middle of the woods that I understand where we're going. The roof of the old amphitheater looms beyond the building; through banks of pine, I can see its concrete tiers almost completely obscured by fallen leaves and branches. "No one's been here in a long time," I venture, while David fishes for something in his jacket pockets outside a battered metal door.

I melt when he looks at me with those handsome green eyes. "We're here," he announces, brandishing a ring of keys. Without hesitation, he shoves one into a padlock, then twists. Another padlock after that, then finally a deadbolt that releases the door. Like a gentleman, he holds it open and gestures me in.

"What is this place?" It's at least ten degrees colder inside the building. There's junk all over the hallway inside—some old loudspeakers, stacks of old LPs, framed photos, countless moldy *Revolutionary Glory* programs, old tricorne hats, and even older boots, mic stands—it's like a crazy yard sale of crap nobody is ever going to want.

David shrugs as he locks the doors behind us and leaves the padlocks on a nearby table. "Old rehearsal hall. Pageant offices. That kind of thing." We're facing each other at last. "My dad was stage manager for the show until it closed. Then he had to retire. So, I kind of grew up running around back here, summers." He tucks the keys away in his pocket, then extends his arm in my direction, palm up. "It kind of broke his heart when the production shut down."

I'm surprised to find my own fingers swinging out

to meet his. His grasp is warm; I actually blush a little. I can't think of a single time anyone's held my hand. It's such a simple thing, but I'd do almost anything to make it last. "So were you one of those kids on stage yelling, *The British are coming?*" I joke.

He looks at me again, very serious, and nods. "Sometimes, yeah. Come on. I want to show you something."

The promise quickens my pulse. With any of the older guys I see, I'd probably retort with something suggestive. David's different, though. "Lead on," is all I say as he tightens his hold and guides me down the hall.

It's getting darker outside. The only windows in this place are set up near the ceiling, under the eaves. Even those are half overgrown with ivy. Beyond the glass, tree branches obscure the evening sky. "Don't worry," he says to me. David's voice is soft but not in the least feminine. "No one ever comes here."

"You must bring a lot of guys to this place, huh?" I regret the words the minute they fly out of my mouth. It's none of my business if he does.

When he drops my hand, I worry I've said the wrong thing. But he's searching for the keys in his pocket. "No." He addresses me over his shoulder as he opens another door. "Only you."

Once again, he presses his palm to mine and pulls me inside what once must have been a dressing room. It's a cavernous space piled with so much furniture that it's difficult to pick out where one piece ends and another begins. Cheap wooden dressing tables with attached mirrors, once white, now battered and worn, have been piled every which way. A barricade of them occupies the far wall, their sockets emptied of the bulbs that once lit up the pageant actors while they applied their stage makeup. Mirrors loom everywhere —all around the room's perimeter, angled in teetering stacks up high, low against the floor. I spy angles and slices of myself no matter where I look.

There's a glow near the room's center that I recognize as an electric space heater, plugged in with extension cords and blowing a warmth that takes the edge off the room's icy neglect. Next to an old sofa, covered in a clean picnic blanket, David has taken the trouble to screw a half dozen lightbulbs in a pair of dressing tables. They're not a strong wattage, and they shed more shadows than light, but among the multiplicity of mirrors, six points of light become twelve, then twenty, a hundred, and more. Seeming thousands of reflected incandescent pinpoints bring the space alive. David and I stand next to each other, hand in hand, wandering among a maze of dim stars.

"What did you do?" I gawk.

"Do you like it?" We're closer than we've ever been —even closer than when I'd sat next to him in the truck that morning.

"It's beautiful. But why?" I'm honestly too overcome to say anything coherent.

He shrugs and takes my other hand. We face each other, fingers intertwined. It feels so good. "Does no one ever do anything for you just because they can?"

I open my mouth to retort but then shut it again. He's asked a fair question. "No?"

He rests his forehead against mine. I relax against him, inhaling his scents of mingled Crest toothpaste and Prell. All I want is to close my eyes and let him take me where he wills. "That seems like a real shame," he says, letting go of my hands. I feel him trundle me out of my track jacket, then allow him to yank my white tee over my head. I shiver, but only because once more, I'm half-naked before him. The heater blows warm air across my torso from behind. "You need someone taking care of you."

I don't. I've always taken care of myself. My lips part to tell him so, but he's shucking his jacket and unzipping the hoodie, then using my own hands to help him skim out of the battered orange raglan beneath. I could tell he was slim, even beneath multiple layers of bulky clothing. These lean hips come as no surprise. His shoulders, though, are broader than I might have believed; he's got the solid, angled physique of a swimmer. A layer of thin hair, the same copper color as his head, covers his pectorals. When I lay a palm on his chest—to see if he's even real—his skin is hot to the touch. "I do," is what comes out of my stammering mouth. "I need someone...doing, you know. The taking care thing."

His mouth brushes my skin, just below the clavicle. I gasp slightly at the friction of his lips across my pec, the unexpected blossom of warm breath, and the flick of his wet tongue on my nipple. His chin presses hard at the base of my ribcage. Then he's on his knees on the concrete floor before me, tugging at the knotted cord holding up my sweats. "I can be that guy." His breath stirs the hairs on my abdomen. "If you want."

My pants hit the floor. Oh, I want. I'm dimly aware of him pulling wide the elastic around my ankles, helping me navigate my high tops through the opening. Then I feel his fingers tug at the waistband of my briefs until they, too, join the rest of my clothes in a pile nearby. In the room's chill, my dick leaps into the air, demanding to be heeded. I can barely stay upright on my feet.

His fingers, still warm, tug at my scrotum. I can't help but moan slightly when they close around my right testicle and squeeze. His nose nuzzles in the cleft where hip meets thigh; I rest my hands atop his fine red hair. Then his hands isolate and compress my other nut.

"Hang on," I say, opening one eye and looking down. "Um...are you doing a testicle check to see if I've shot a load?"

David snickers like a mischievous kid as he rises. "M.J. did that to you, too, huh?"

"Dude. It's a sickness with him." I join in his laughter. I might have said more, but now we're face to face, David has other things in mind. His fingers reach out and clamp down on my nipples, tweaking them expertly between his thumbs and fingertips. My lids narrow to slits as sensations overwhelm me—the electric intensity of his tweaking digits, the red glow of the heater on my backside contrasting the room's chilliness on my front, the moist pressure of his lips against my forehead, my cheek, my ear. The room spins. All those points of light whirl. Everywhere I look, I see images of the two of us, reflected and splintered among this funhouse of dressing room mirrors.

Dizzy and disoriented, I'm certain I'm falling. But no, David has lowered me onto the sofa. He won't let me come to any harm. My backside feels every spring and hole through the blanket, but I don't care. He could arrange me on sacks of potatoes, so long as he keeps staring at me with those big green eyes. I watch as he kicks off his boots, unbuckles his belt, and slips out of his jeans. He wears a pair of red briefs—way fancier than my white BVDs—but not for long. He's so erect that he has difficulty stretching the waistband over the tent, distending the colored cotton, but soon they fall to his ankles. Save for my sneakers and his socks, we're both now nude.

And as red as the briefs were, they're nothing in comparison to the deep, angry scarlet of the cock underneath. I almost gasp at the sight of those seven or so inches that angle up and away from his hips; the head, covered with folds of foreskin I don't often see here in the South, looks enraged. He's already leaking precum. I lurch from my reclining position and, like a greedy kid on Christmas, make a grab.

"Not yet," he says, stopping me with a palm to the chest. When I huff impotent whimpers of frustration, he pushes me back down. "Soon. My turn, first."

My own cock has been stiff since we entered the place. It seems like weeks since it last got any attention —though it's only been since Thursday. Still, when David wraps one of his hands around the base and points it at his open mouth, it leaps and throbs. "Please," I beg, wanting nothing more than to feel his lips around me. But then, when I feel the hot breath from his open mouth sear my flesh, I yank away and attempt to hold him at arm's length. "You don't have to," I tell him.

I must sound like a psycho. It's weird how guilty and mixed up I feel. I want him so badly, but at the same time, I'm almost ashamed to accept pleasure instead of providing it. He settles me down once more, though, pushing me back against the sofa's arm and leaning on my stomach as if to keep me still. "But I want to. Let me enjoy myself," he whispers.

Who am I to deny him?

He wants to kiss me, first. Honestly, I'd be content to spend the afternoon with his lips pressing hard against mine, his tongue exploring the furthest recesses of my mouth. His furry chest grinds against my smooth skin, causing such delicious discomfort that I gasp; my cock lunges and thrusts for him while he answers with a riposte that pins me to the sofa. It is the sweetest skirmish in which I've ever engaged.

Eventually, I surrender. He shoves me into the upholstery with one hand and holds me there, not letting me rise again, as he forces apart my knees. I can only sneak short glimpses as he wraps his fingers around the base of my meat and begins devouring it. Watching him doubles the sensations; lingering too long on the sight of my cock distending his cheeks, on the shimmer of his hair falling in a fringe over my demanding erection might bring me to the brink. I don't want the pleasure with which he's lavishing me to end. Not yet. Safer to clamp shut my lids and only imagine that handsome face looking up.

My fear of shooting quickly passes. Even though my cock is a poker, white-hot in the furnace of David's mouth, and even though his slobber courses down my balls in runnels that tickle and thrill, I remain rigid in his expert grasp. When I open my eyes once more, he's licking up and down my length with his tongue flat and wide, staring at me from down on the floor while I tremble and shudder. How the fuck did a little shit like me hit the jackpot today?

"I want to remember this forever," I whisper to him, letting the back of my index finger trace his jaw. "I don't want it to end."

He batters himself with my cock. It slaps against his nose and eye socket with a wet smack. "But it's happening right now," he says, grinning at me. "Just enjoy it, silly."

I laugh as again he tenderizes his face with my mallet. "Let me do something for you, though," I beg. "I feel so selfish."

He spits on his hand and adds the moisture to my already-slick cock, causing it to leap and swell. It was red before; now it burns an angry scarlet. "What would you do for me?"

"Anything."

"Anything?" There's a mischievous quirk to his lips as he squeezes and paws at my shaft. "Dangerous offer."

"Seriously." My voice is a raspy echo in the cavern of this room. I'd make a Faustian bargain to keep David happy. "Anything."

Luckily, he doesn't demand my soul. Instead, he stands up and looms above me, his uncut knob straining to the right. I clamber up from my reclining position, dick pronging, legs spread, arms hanging heavily between them. With the sex-addled expression on my face, I feel and probably look like a big dumb gorilla. I watch, jaw agape, as slowly David turns. He's wearing nothing but that pair of white work socks, their soles dark gray from the dirty concrete. Like a cat in the sun, he stretches, arching his back and showing me the quantities of red fur springing from the center of his chest and spilling down his torso toward his hips; I admire the glow of the light reflected upon both his armpit hair and the white planes of his skin. Smiling, he shows off one hip and then the other. His round and pert little butt shakes with a lascivious wiggle as it passes.

"Know what I want?" he asks once he's facing me again. I shake my head. My lips and throat are too dry to summon more than a croak. "I want you to lay me down." He edges closer, then lowers himself onto the sofa, next to me. "I want you to spread my legs." David grasps my cock, giving it a firm squeeze that makes it spit forth a glob of goo. "I want you to spit on my hole." Now he all but shoves me from my seat so that he can kneel on the furniture's edge. The picnic blanket collapses from the back into a heap at his hands. "And I want you to fuck me blind."

I'm almost breathless from his sexy enticements, but I'm a little taken aback. "You want me to...?" I gesture toward his rear end. He nods. "It's just that I've never..."

"You've never done anal?"

I can't lose face with him. Not now. "I've done lots of anal," I protest. "Loads. All the time. Here an anal. There an anal. I'm Old McAnal." I consider whether I sound like some kind of sex maniac. "It's just that I've never...you know. I've never been the...Greek active."

"Greek active?" He's staring at me with his laughter barely suppressed. "Are you Mediterranean?"

"No!"

"Is it a weird fraternity thing?"

"Greek active is what guys call it when you're the— you know!" Here, I thought I was some kind of sexual sophisticate, but it's funny how easily he makes me feel like a dope. "When you put it in, instead of take it."

"Ohhhh." I can't tell whether I want to wipe the chuckle from his pretty lips or kiss it away. "You've never been the guy who puts it in. You've only..."

"Been Greek passive." We're both laughing now. I can't help it—I've never spoken about this stuff out loud. I've only done the actual deeds in toilets and parks and in the backs of cars and alleys and the occasional bedroom. I can only hope I'm charming him with my naivety more than turning him off with ignorance. "I haven't..."

"Yeah, yeah, I get it." He's risen to stand and face me. I'm not sure what to call it when you're having a weird, funny conversation in the middle of sex with a guy, yet you're both hard as bricks—but I'm digging it. A lot. "But come on. You know how it works."

"Well, sure."

Taking a chance, he spins away from me and nudges his ass in my direction. He reaches around and guides my stiff dick into the lightly hairy cleft. "Maybe the idea of fucking me turns you off?"

Even though I've never been in a guy's hole before, my cock jerks and twitches at the thought as it grazes his cheeks. "No," I choke out. "It definitely doesn't turn me off."

"Well, how about it, then?" His gaze is steady over his shoulder as he kneels once more on the sofa. His cheeks part to reveal a pink hole made even redder by the whorl of fine hair within. I can barely control my breathing. "How about you Greek active me harder than anyone's Greek active-d me before? Huh?"

"You are a goof," I say, rolling my eyes. A genuine smile widens my mouth.

"C'mon, Greek boy." He slaps his ass, grabs his right cheek, and spreads it wide. "*Opa!*"

"On behalf of all my fellow island residents of the birthplace of democracy, I object to your crude..."

"Yeah, yeah, I took Civics 101, too." He slaps his ass, serious once more. "I mean it. Fuck me, Wick. Fuck my ass."

The hard edge to his voice turns me on. It's making me want to do things. Never has anyone desired me this much. Not in this particular way. Deep at the root of my dick, there's a weird sensation I haven't felt before—a vibration, deep inside. All its nerves jangle like they've been struck with a tuning fork. I don't know what's holding me back. Even the way David says my name makes me want his hole. How difficult could it be?

"I want you inside, Wickham. Fuck me." His lips force out one more set of silent syllables: *Fuck me.*

"Would it make you happy?" I probe at his hole with two fingers of my right hand, surprised at how warm and moist it already is back there. I'm not trying to tease him. I genuinely want to know.

He must sense my sincerity because he half-twists around to face me. "Having you fill me? Nothing else in this or any other world would make me happier."

I suck thoughtfully on my index and middle finger, spit on a little extra, and push. Not deep. Just a knuckle's worth. "I do want to make you happy."

"Yes." He's gasping now. His hips gyrate as he tries to engulf more of my fingers. "Make me happy."

"I guess I said I'd do anything, huh?" More spit. More of my fingers, this time two knuckles in. I'm astonished how easily he opens, how slippery a little saliva makes him. My own hole twitches in sympathy. "Anything you want."

"That's what you said." His voice is barely audible now. David arches his spine and lifts his ass high into the air. His head hangs low, so that he speaks into the sofa cushion. "You promised. I want you deep inside. Fucking my hole."

"Well." Now, I'm teasing. I don't believe I've ever had this effect on anyone. It's incendiary how much he wants me. Kneeling on the creaky furniture, legs spread wide, shoulders pressed against the sofa's rear, he's not just ready—he's eager. My dick leaps in the direction of the kid's hole as I draw closer. I've got another handful of spit ready to slather along my joystick. The head glistens from the extra lube. "A promise is a promise."

At the sensation of my flesh nudging his hole,

David lets out a feral groan from deep in his chest. "Wick, you are *torturing* me."

"Nah." I know to go slow at first—or at least, that's how I like guys to start with me. Some sadistic side I've never encountered before, though, makes me shove in the first couple of inches. He reacts with a yelp. I don't encounter any real resistance, though. I know I haven't hurt him. "I'm gonna make you feel good, baby." I slide in a little more. "Trust me."

All I get for an answer is a deep sigh of contentment.

No one has ever told me how good fucking ass feels. The warmth is incredible. The wetness is wild. Sure, I'd used some spit, but it feels as if David is producing lube enough for the both of us. Filling a hole is hot enough on its own, I'm finding. But knowing that it's David I'm sliding into makes my head spin and my knees buckle. I have to grab onto the nearest dressing table for support by the time I slide in that last, deepest inch.

Now I'm all the way in. I feel his butt connect with my pelvis. "How'm I doing?"

"So good." I can't tell whether he's sobbing or laughing, but the catch in his lungs makes my dick even harder. "You feel so good, baby."

A minute before, when I'd called him *baby*, I'd worried about how he might react to a casual endearment. It had just slipped out, is all. Hearing it back sends a flush of heat throughout my body, starting from my thudding heart and spreading to every extremity. My dick swells once more, making him groan. Some primal instinct, deep within, sets my hips into motion. I grind, withdraw, and again grind my dick deep inside his pulsating hole, over and over. It feels so good and natural that it's a minute before a coherent thought forms: I'm doing it. I'm actually fucking David's hole. "I like when you call me that," I confide.

He raises his head and sniffs deeply, as if his nose has been running. "I will call you my baby every time you fuck me," he promises. "But that means you'll need to keep fucking me."

"I'll definitely keep fucking you," I vow. When I thrust harder, he bites his lip, closes his eyes, and allows savage satisfaction to shine from his crooked grin. "You gonna keep putting this pretty ass in the air for me?"

"Oh, god. As much as you need." My attempt at dirty talk is working on him. Knowing I'm turning him on only makes me fuck harder. "Fuck it every day of the week, Wick." Every time I slide in or out, his hole lets out a wet squelch. Maybe he really is self-lubricating, or maybe I'm just pumping out enough precum to keep him slippery. Either way, I love how sexy it feels. "You can own my ass if you want."

"You want me to own it? You want it to be all mine?" The things he says drive me wild. I rabbit in and out. I'm turned on enough to give his butt an experimental slap. The sound of hand clapping ass fills the room, quickly followed by his appreciative grunt. I strike again, this time a lot harder. The smack prompts him to drive his hips backward, meeting me thrust for thrust. My pulse quickens. "So, I'm making you feel good, baby?"

"You are Greek active-ing the fuck out of me," he says, barely able to get out the words. Then, without warning, he pulls his ass off my cock and stands.

Denied the novelty I've enjoyed, I whine with frustration. But David grabs me by the shoulders, wheels me around, and plants my naked butt so firmly on the sofa that I wince as one of its broken springs attempts to give me a rectal exam. His knees straddle mine. Looking directly at me, he clamps one hand around my cock, lowers himself down, and guides me inside him once more. "Oh, fuck," I whisper, locking eyes. His tight hole slithers down my shaft until he's impaled deeply. "I love that ass so much."

"Remember, you own this ass, baby," he replies.

My head lolls atop the sofa's back as I look into his face. I try to thrust, but he's in control now. I've tried to sit on guys' dicks in the past, and I'll be honest: I've never been that great at it. David, though, is a pro. He knows just how to rotate his hips to hit the good spot, the spot where my head bangs his prostate, the spot I want to keep ramming until one of us cries uncle. Every time he twists and buckles, I grunt, whimper, or let out a wordless lament from deep in my core. When I reach up to twist his nipples and make him wince and nod for more mistreatment, it's as if I'm taking sweet revenge.

This is how it goes for several minutes more, staring into each other's eyes while he whets my weapon on his grindstone, teasing and torturing each other. When we can resist no longer, we kiss for long and passionate minutes, filling the starlit room with murmurs and sighs. I still feel selfish, sitting here, pinned to the sofa by my lover as he gifts me such extravagant pleasure, but I can't protest. The red flush on his chest tells me that he's extracting his own gratification; the gluttonous way his hole pistons my dick lets me know he's just as greedy. What strange arithmetic this is, adding our individual bliss into a sum exponentially larger and infinitely more abundant than either of us. I'd be content to hide away here, in our secret sanctuary, fucking David as days and seasons pass.

In fact, I have no idea how much time has elapsed when David next speaks. "Why do you see him?"

I'm so high from raw sensation that it takes a minute for the question to register. "M.J.?"

He nods, continuing to stretch his hole over my cock. "Is it the gifts?" I must appear shamefaced at his bluntness. All I can think of is that lapful of gift boxes in David's truck this morning. "Listen, it's okay. He gave me stuff, too."

My arms flop helplessly. "Yeah, kinda. I mean, his presents are usually shit, but..."

"Expensive shit," David supplies. He understands. Why are we having this conversation now, though? M.J. is the last person I want to think about. "I can't give you gifts, Wick."

No. No, he can't think that's all I care about. "I don't want gifts from you."

"Is it the attention?" His eyes bore into mine. "Because if you like attention, I've got plenty."

I hold the redhead's face between my hands and say in my most serious and least-ever smart-aleck voice, "I don't have to see M.J. again. M.J. isn't serious. He's just—" I hate having to defend that weird and misjudged relationship. Especially after yesterday, when the professor's tantrum had clearly spelled its end.

"Convenient?" David supplies. There's relief in his expression. Even though he's two years my elder, and even though we're doing some of the most adult stuff imaginable, his happy reaction to my responses makes me want to gather the kid in my arms and protect him from harm. "Can I be your convenience, instead?"

"No. Never," I breathe. I kiss his chin, his pouty

lips, his eyes, his forehead. "David, be something way better than that."

After a long silence, during which his hips never stop moving, he nods. Then, with vicious intent, he stabs his hole down to the base of my dick. I gasp and stiffen. "This load is mine." There's a sneer on his face that's half ecstatic, half cruel. "I've earned it. You're going to give it to me."

"Yes, sir," I respond, equally alarmed and turned on by his intensity.

"The first load you ever fucked in a hole." I nod in confirmation. "And I'm the lucky guy who gets it."

"I think we're both—" I start to say, but his hungry mouth smothers my reply.

I'm starved of air as he forces his tongue between my lips. He's slamming me now with that ass, withdrawing and plunging down on my shaft with such force that I worry he'll get the angle wrong and break it in half. His aim is impeccable, though. His gravity flattens my balls with every descent of his weight upon them, but I welcome the pain.

"I can't last much longer," I plead. I'm trapped without knowing which way to go, never wanting this pleasure to end, but needing it to.

He makes the decision in the end. "Give it to me," he demands, as he crashes down and clenches his hole as tightly as possible. Again. "Give it to me." Yet again. "It's mine, baby. All mine."

What can I do but surrender? Waves of electricity ebb and flow throughout my body. Usually, when I shoot, it's an explosion, sharp and distinct from the build-up before. This time, though, is different. I know I'm climaxing. I can feel my balls contract and expand, sense the wetness of his hole as I unload inside. The accompanying pleasure is a blossoming—the correct and beautiful flow from one natural state into another. A sweet culmination that leaves me gasping for air. Then, as he keeps milking from me every last drop, a slow continuation.

Eventually, my senses return. I find myself sweaty and panting. "Baby," I whisper, giving myself the pleasure of calling him that one more time. Hopefully, it won't be the last.

His jaw juts sideways. I've never seen him so cocky. Exercising the victor's prerogative, he continues pleasuring himself on my still-rigid meat. His own side-leaning dick fills his left hand. He squeezes tightly, choking it. Three quick strokes, followed by three more, and then he blows. A rope of hot semen ejects from David's hooded tip, spattering both onto my chin and the back of the sofa. A second and third jet hit my chest. The rest oozes out slowly, dribbling down his crooked shaft as he jerks and bucks atop me.

"Wickham." Now that his shudders have subsided, David's voice is hushed. His fingers stroke my cheek, just as they had the first time I'd seen him early that morning. It takes him a moment to recuperate. When his eyes finally open, he regards me with alarm. "That was...amazing. But I shouldn't have made you—"

I shake my head and silence his protest. He doesn't need to explain. He definitely doesn't need to apologize. I pull him to me in a kiss as my cock slops out of his wet, used hole. Then, tenderly, I settle him down and curl us into a ball on that uncomfortable sofa. For long minutes, we hang onto each other, listening to the steady wheeze of the heater and the Morse code of pine branches against the windows high above.

When he speaks again, there's no hint of regret. "I was thinking that maybe, if you wanted, we could get something to eat. Together. Pizza? Stromboli? A burger? What's your pleasure?"

He's offering me an out, I realize. An easy escape. This is the one time, though, when I have absolutely no desire to pull up my sweats and run for it. "When you say together...would I have to walk twenty feet behind you?" His eyes roll, and he lets loose a grin as he shakes his head. "I could maybe even talk to you?"

"You can always talk to me, Wick."

"Even in public?" I sound shyer than I intend.

He kisses the back of my hand. "In front of the whole world."

My breath catches a little. I hadn't realized until now exactly how much I want what he offered. "I do like pizza," I concede.

He tries to sit up. "Should we?"

"Not yet." I push my lover down, shaking my head. "The pizza place will still be there in a few minutes," I whisper, moving in for a kiss. "We'll go when we're ready."

He snuggles close. "Five more minutes."

"Five more minutes," I agree.

But I know here, in this magical lair David has prepared for the two of us, among these many mirrors, the five minutes will become ten. The ten, twenty. The twenty, forty—like the lights and the images of our interlocked limbs in the mirrors, forever multiplying.

THE TEAROOM IN THE TREES

by Peter Schutes

THE TEAROOM IN THE TREES

The Tearoom in the Trees

My California college was in a big city. It was a commuter school and had very little campus life. I took the streetcar to school three times a week for some semesters and twice a week for others. But when I decided to study French, I was there every day. Classes were one hour Monday through Friday in the afternoon. They were held in an old, asbestos-filled earthquake trap of a Humanities building. The University officers knew they had to get rid of it at some point, so they began migrating classes to other buildings while they built a shiny new Humanities building in a new location.

The language classes were among the last to leave the building, mainly because there was a language lab there, and it would be hard to re-create it in another location. Five days a week, I took the train to campus and sat in a nearly empty building, learning to pronounce "Qu'est-ce que c'est" and "Je ne sais pas."

If you have been to college, you don't have to imagine what the restrooms are like on the top floor of a mostly empty building. Once the English department moved out, they became de facto bathhouses. I was timid, but I eventually gave in to the temptation. I'm a lousy cocksucker, but I let the boys suck me off during break and after class. The whole top floor was empty, so only men with a single purpose ever used that tearoom.

My real passion was getting fucked in the ass. There was plenty of buttfucking in that bathroom, but I was so wishy-washy that I never once took it up the ass in there. I watched in envy as the pushy bottoms took their fill of cum in the rear. I'd learned early on that I was too big, even for the greediest bottoms. Any time a foolish man with eyes bigger than his ass rubbed up against my crotch, I pushed him away and said, "You can't handle this." I was right. Spit wasn't enough, and lube was hard to come by. Even with a thick slathering of greasy Crisco, I couldn't get in more than the tip. Some men are built for a fast fuck. I wasn't. My cock wasn't built to top another man because it was just too damned huge. I didn't want to anyway. Like I said, I was a bottom.

Once in a great while, I would see an older student come in. He was a bodybuilder with black hair and light blue eyes. He had a Middle Eastern accent. He was a total anal top. I wanted him badly, but my shyness always won out. The aggressive bottoms would elbow their way to him and push him into a stall. Aggressive cocksuckers would wait for me to finish peeing. As I shook off my long, fat cock after a much-needed piss, they would grab it and try to swallow it. As always, they just ended up putting both hands on the shaft and nursed the head until I came. I never got a deep-throat blow job. I didn't miss it because I'd never had one. I liked coming in another man's mouth; that was good enough.

On the rare occasion when the bodybuilder was in there, I came quickly. He was a verbal top, and he fucked hard. His bottom's moans would fill the air. He was very verbal. His tirades were filled with "yeah's," "fucks," and "you like that, don't you little faggots." It was so hot, my balls would boil and erupt in less than a minute. I'd feed my cocksucker, zip up, and return to class before the ten-minute break was through. On days when he wasn't there, it took longer. I'd usually have time to blow my load, but not always. I dreaded those days when I'd return to class with a raging boner, hiding it as best I could. I always sat in the back of the class. As I conjugated verbs, my hardon would subside. I could never be sure, but I'd like to think that nobody saw my long fat cock hanging down one leg, a wet spot at the end. They certainly never said anything to my face.

The bodybuilder stopped coming around. It was a huge disappointment. I didn't see him for months.

One day, I was walking in the shopping district, and I needed a piss. The hotels that lined the square were always the best places to go. Department stores had taken to requiring keys, but the hotel bathrooms were wide open.

The restroom at the Hilton was empty when I went in, but then I heard the door creak. A man went into the stall and locked it. I heard him fart. As I was washing my hands, the man came out. It was the bodybuilder. He walked to the sink beside me, checking me out.

"You're a top, aren't you?"

I blushed and shook my head.

"Why not?"

His eyes widened as I grabbed the leg of my pants, pinching my long, thick flesh between my thumb and forefinger as I ran it up and down the length.

I said, "That's why not."

He said, "Here, feel this." He bent his arm, and his bicep bulged. I wrapped both hands around it, but my fingers barely touched. "It's big, no?"

"Yeah, huge."

He put one hand around my arm and squeezed. "I want to fuck you. You're a weak little boy."

I didn't mind the insult. It was the truth.

"Come on." He grabbed my hand and dragged me out of the bathroom. "This place is full of cops. Let's go somewhere better."

I was surprised when we got to the parking lot. He had valet parked, which cost a fortune. The car pulled up. It was a Ferrari GTO.

The muscleman was an aggressive driver. He roared through the city streets towards the park. As he went, he cursed out other drivers and cut them off, slamming on his brakes to annoy them. I'd never been in a high-performance car before. I thought I would hate it, but he was so fucking masculine, it made me horny. I rubbed my long cock through my jeans. At a stoplight, he caught me rubbing off and slapped my hand.

"You wait, bitch. Wait until I'm fucking you." I melted hearing him trash-talk me. I wanted him badly.

We got to the park; he parked his Ferrari in the red next to a copse of trees.

I said, "You'll get a ticket."

He shrugged. "I don't give a fuck. I can afford it."

Everything about this guy was hot. I wanted to know more.

"What's your name?" I thought maybe I'd recognize what billionaire family he came from. I came from old money, but our branch of the family wasn't rich anymore. Still, I knew the social register and the names in there. I figured he must be a Saudi prince or something.

"No fucking names, bitch." He shut me down. I wasn't sure if I wanted to know who he was. Maybe he was an arms dealer or part of some Persian cartel. I didn't want to wind up buried in a ditch, so I obeyed him. No more questions.

He took me by the wrist and dragged me into the pine grove. There was a well-worn path, but he turned down a trail that was scarcely visible to the naked eye. As we wound down the path, I saw guys leaning with one foot up against a tree, or sucking, or fucking. It was a room in the wilderness. I had heard about these places but never knew where they were until Mr. Muscles brought me there that day.

We turned off the narrow path and into the wildflowers. I knew it was probably illegal to walk there, but I didn't think it was quite as serious an infraction as what we were about to do.

There was a log lying on its side. He pushed me hard on the back until I was bent over, pinned to the log. I heard the rustle of his pants as he dropped them. I tried to catch a glimpse of his cock, but he was already crouched down, his massive thighs hiding his prize.

"Don't turn around." He pressed his nose to my crack and pressed his tongue against my hole until it yielded and let him in. I shivered as he ran his thick tongue around my anus, coating it with thick, syrupy spit. Like the rest of his body, his tongue was big and thick. He clamped his lips onto my butthole and pushed more and more spit into the hole.

When I was dripping with spit, he pulled back and stood. I turned my head and saw him spit into his hand and rub his cock. It wasn't as big as mine, nobody's was, but it was plenty big. I think maybe eight inches long, and mercifully, only five inches around on the shaft. The perfect size.

"What did I say, faggot? Don't turn around." I didn't need to. I had all the information I needed now. It was going to hurt at first, but then it was going to be perfect.

The blue-eyed man pressed his mushroom head against my hole.

"You ready?" It was a brief moment of tender concern in his otherwise brutal manner.

I nodded. He pushed, and I saw stars. His cock head was flared. When he drove past my sphincter, it made a loud pop. I wanted him to wait there for the pain to subside, but I had a pretty good idea of what would happen if I asked him for anything. He was a brutal fuck, and it would be worse if I spoke.

"Oh, fuck, that feels good. Oh yeah, you're my little bitch."

I fought the urge to squirm as his long cock slid inside me and landed hard against the back wall. With expert technique, he lifted my left hip and pushed past the inner hole with another loud pop. I'd bottomed with enough big guys to know how to relax and let it happen. His corona was probably six and a half inches around, and it hurt. I let out a yelp.

"Take it, bitch. I wanna hear you moan."

I moaned. I sighed. I let him in completely with a groan.

Roughly, he pulled back. Another loud pop came as he left my colon, dragging his fat head through my shitter until he landed at my prostate gland. He took tiny strokes there, waiting for my huge cock to release a dribble of precum. His hand was there to catch it. I heard him slurp it up.

"Your boy juice is sweet. And your cock is so big. Make it smaller."

I had a raging hard-on, and there was nothing I could do to make it any smaller. I was a grower and a shower. Even soft, I was probably bigger than him hard.

"I can't."

He slapped me. It only made my hard cock throb.

"Hide that disgusting cock with both hands."

I did as he asked. I rubbed it, but he said, "No!"

I tried to cover one thumb with the other palm so I could rub just a little, but he caught me. It pissed him off.

In a rage, he pounded my hole from stem to stern. My cock dribbled a long stream onto the dirt at my feet. He caught some more and sucked it down.

"Yeah, little bitch, you like my big cock inside you, don't you?"

"Uh-huh."

"Say it!"

I said, "I like your big cock inside me, sir."

Those were the magic words. He pounded me furiously, his breath coming in short bursts. Then he stopped.

"I don't want to come yet." His sweat dripped onto my back. It was so full of testosterone, I thought I'd grow muscles through osmosis. He smelled musky. It wasn't cologne. He gave off raging hormones like a bull in an arena.

My asshole twitched and tightened around his cock. He slapped my ass hard, and it tightened.

"You gonna jerk me off with your ass, eh?" He

slapped me again. I squeezed involuntarily. He chuckled. "I love to cum like this." Harder and faster, he spanked me until I spasmed. Now my ass contracted over and over without any prompting. He leaned back and sighed.

"Oh yeah, good little pussy boy. Jerk me off." He slid slowly back and forth as my ass muscles brought him closer to orgasm. I yearned for his cock to push past that inner hole again, so I pressed back, and it popped inside.

"Oh shit, you like it, don't you?" He held my hips and jackhammered my insides, his breath growing harder and shorter as his cock grew harder and longer.

"Get ready, faggot. I'm giving you my cum." He said it between gasps.

"Give it to me." He was too far gone to care that I'd given him an order. The spit was drying out, and I was praying for him to cum.

"Oh shit! Oh fuck!" He switched languages and said curses in Arabic and French. "Merde!" That was all I recognized.

Then, in a frenzy, he unleashed a hot river deep in my colon. He held himself tightly against me, his hips crushing my round butt cheeks. The tide of cum continued to flow. He collapsed on my back, his manly sweat mingling with mine. I felt his hot breath on my neck.

He said, "Don't expect me to kiss you." But then he licked behind my ear before putting his full lips on my neck. He sucked until I knew there would be a hickey. It didn't hurt, but it was rough. He kissed my cheek, then turned my head and locked lips with me. I expected his tongue to invade my mouth, but he waited for me. Hesitantly, I pressed my tongue against his, licking the roof of his mouth. He yielded, passive. As cum dribbled out of my bare ass, we kissed passionately.

He pulled away. "Now you do me."

I laughed. He looked hurt. "You don't want to fuck me?"

His personality changed completely. Suddenly, he was a submissive, whiny bitch. It was as if he had a split personality. Maybe he did.

"I can't fuck you," I said, "It's too big."

He laughed. "I'm a fucking bodybuilder. I have complete control over every muscle. I've taken arms the size of legs."

He lay down on a bed of pine needles and raised his ass. The edge of his hole hung loose like a pouty vagina. His big cock was soft now, and it lolled from side to side, maybe three inches long. His balls were big, and they made his cock look even smaller.

I said, "We don't have enough lube."

He said, "I put in Crisco before I left the house."

I cautiously put a finger in his loose hole; sure enough, it was slick with grease. I put in two fingers, then three.

He moaned. "Oh, yes, do me."

God's honest truth: I had never topped before. Nobody would have me once they saw what was between my legs. Until now, I had never wanted to. But with this brutal assfucker begging for my cock, I felt my semi-hard monster swell. I wanted to make him scream.

He lay on his back with his knees to his ears. I knelt in the pine needles, lifting my cock until it was in line with his butthole. I crawled forward on my knees until it rested against the loose opening. I pressed in the first half inch of flesh. My cock head is nine inches around at the corona and four inches long, no joke. The shaft is ten by seven. My cock is 14 inches long, probably the only one of its kind. You can call bullshit all you want; I know what I've got.

"Fuck me now! Hard! Stick it in me!"

I smiled. "Shut the fuck up, faggot."

His eyes widened as he grinned.

He started to say something, but I shook my head. "Silence."

He nodded obediently. His submission made my cock throb harder.

I pushed against the hole, but it didn't let me in. I took another crawl forward on my knees, and the pressure made my cock buckle. I pressed my hips forward, and the tip pushed in another half inch.

The muscleman grabbed his ass cheeks and pulled them apart, letting another inch of cock head into him. I saw tears in the corner of his eyes.

He said, "What are you waiting for?"

If I were close enough, I would have slapped his face. I could barely reach his ass cheek, but I slapped it hard. Suddenly, he released, and my head pushed past the loose opening with a slurping sound. Once my head passed, I pushed to the back, gliding on the greasy shortening.

I watched his face as I moved through him. He looked like he was deadlifting three hundred pounds, but he still had a smile.

Like a woman, he moaned softly in a high pitch. "Fuck me."

I was close enough now to slap his face. "Shut up! I told you to shut up!"

He threw his head back, clamping his lips together to keep from speaking. He thrashed about, grabbing clumps of pine needles. He twisted his waist, and I suddenly felt that glorious sensation as my head found that second hole. I pushed ahead, surprised by the resistance.

The aggressive top from a few minutes earlier was reduced to a trembling mass of flesh. His abdominal muscles quaked as his whole body shook. He grabbed fistfuls of pine needles.

"Ohhhh! Oui! Nam! Yes!" He rocked his massive body from side to side as my head passed the second hole with a loud "pop!" and slid in further. I still had a few inches to go. I walked forward on my knees until my thighs rested against his massive basketball-shaped ass cheeks. I planted my hands on either side of his head in a push-up position and let gravity drive me the rest of the way inside.

It wasn't enough for him. He held his ass cheeks open, allowing me to push in the final inch. I felt my pubes rub against his loose ass-pussy.

"Fuck me!"

I slapped his face to remind him to keep his mouth shut. Like Downward Dog in Yoga class, I bent at the hips, pulling my cock back out until the head was just inside the lips of his ass. Then gravity rammed me back in, the popping sound filling the air like one hand clapping against itself.

It was my first time fucking, but like a rutting dog, my hips knew what to do. I got back on my knees, hands on his massive pectoral muscles, and thrust hard.

"Pop! Pop! Pop!" I pounded his colon until something mysterious happened. I felt him stroking my cock deep inside. His gut muscles were spasming in waves like he was trying to shit out my dick as I pushed my way in. I stopped for a second and let the oscillation of muscular contractions caress my cock.

The bodybuilder's eyes rolled backward, blinking rapidly. I almost thought I'd given him a seizure, but then he whispered words to himself so softly that I could scarcely hear him. I knew he was conscious.

"You like that?" I was going to allow him one word.

"Yes. Oh please, keep fucking me!"

I slapped him. "Yes or No, faggot!"

That word made him open his eyes, and for a second, I thought I saw a snarl, but he relaxed, nodding. He was a faggot, just like me.

I wanted to take long strokes, but kneeling on the ground, I couldn't angle myself far enough back. My muscle man could tell what I needed and knew what to do. With his powerful arms, he maneuvered until he could pull himself to lie face up across the flat log. Any other man's cock would have fallen out of his ass, but mine stayed inside as I stood. He pulled his knees back to his ears.

With one leg forward, I was able to hinge at the hips and fuck him long and deep. This was better than jacking off or getting blown. I felt wet, greasy flesh encasing and squeezing my whole cock as it rammed into him.

I surveyed his incredible body. Every muscle was defined. He had eight abdominal muscles, tree-trunk thighs, big tits, a strong neck, bulging biceps and triceps, and powerful hands that gripped my arms as I fucked him.

"Ohhhhh. Mmmmm." I let him make those sounds. In truth, I wanted him to talk dirty to me, but I was getting revenge for the way he'd treated me. I decided to let him talk.

In a filthy stream of expletives, he begged me to fuck him.

"Oh please, fuck my pussy. Make me a woman.

Your cock is so fucking huge." He was just as hot begging me to fuck him as he had been when he was fucking me. "Fuck that hole. Make me cum."

I looked down. His little three-inch cock was all grown to its full eight, throbbing in the air like a baby bird reaching for a worm. A thin stream of juice rolled down the head. I caught it and licked it from my finger. It was neither salty nor sweet. It had a flavor like medicine. Maybe that was what anabolic steroids tasted like. It made me want to pound him harder.

Up until that point, I had been oblivious to our surroundings. I thought it was raining when I felt a splash on my back. I looked up to see a circle of men jacking off. I didn't always like being seen while having sex, but this time, I was on top, and it turned me on more. Another splash landed in my hair. Men of all ages, shapes, and sizes were stroking their cocks and watching intently as I turned the bodybuilder inside out with my huge fuck stick.

I wanted them to know just how big I was. I stepped back, letting my cock fall out of his sloppy hole. The crowd gave a collective gasp. I lifted my throbbing member and shoved it back into his ass, walking forward until I was in completely. I heard a groan, and another load of cum landed on me.

The bodybuilder glanced up when a load landed on his face.

He said, "Yeah, you little-dicked motherfuckers. Watch me get fucked by his huge cock."

A man with a very big cock stepped forward and said, "Shut your hole, or I'll shut it for you."

The muscleman opened his mouth expectantly, and the big-dicked spectator became a performer. He forced his way down his throat. My muscular fuck toy was plugged now at both ends. He greedily slurped and sucked the big man's meat. I could see the outline of the cock as it slid in and out of his throat.

More and more men came to the clearing and began jacking off. A few jacked each other off. We were more popular than a three-ring circus. A three-man performance under the big top.

As more people appeared and more men shot their loads, I got closer to coming. It was when the other guy came in the muscle man's throat that I started to cross over the edge. I stopped, but the waves of contractions kept stroking my cock. The man stepped back, letting my bodybuilder lift his head, cum dribbling from the edges of his mouth. His piercing blue eyes met mine. He reached until I understood he wanted to kiss. I leaned over and tasted the cum in his mouth. Our tongues fought for dominance while we guzzled the shared load of cum. He brought one hand up and held my head from behind, keeping me locked in the drippy kiss. He exhaled through his nose, tickling my face with his hot breath.

That connection completed the circuit. It put me over. I pulled back and said, "Shit! I'm gonna come."

He said, "Come inside me! Oui! Yes! Come inside me."

In long strokes, I coursed in and out of his guts, faster, harder, until the one-hand clapping noise became a round of applause. Pop! Pop! As I plunged into his colon and back out again, the air began to fill with the cum of a dozen men. It was a downpour of manly juices.

My massive balls pulled up against my thick shaft, and I felt the tingle of an impending release.

"Take it, bitch!" And he did. I came harder than I'd ever come before. In spurt after endless spurt, my semen flooded his guts. The popping sound became a soft slurping noise as I fucked my juices deeper inside him. After the tenth or eleventh squirt, I collapsed on his broad chest, resting my cheeks against his firm breast. He stroked my hair, making soft noises and whispering to me in Arabic or Farsi or whatever language that was. The white rain kept falling as I lay with his bulging arms wrapped around my shoulders. He pressed his tongue behind my ear and nibbled my earlobe. I softened a little but stayed firmly wedged up his rear.

"You have ruined me. No one will ever be big enough." I relished those words. As much as my cock had been a hindrance, the thought that I had conquered this vain macho man and spoiled his sex life forever after was a big turn-on. I felt my cock swell inside him.

His eyes widened. "You will fuck me again?"

"It'll take longer."

He said, "First, I must fuck you again. We take turns."

I felt his throbbing cock pressing against my abdomen. He was ready for another round. My ass was sore but not unwilling.

I grinned and kissed his cheek. "Okay, let's give these guys another show."

***

I asked him, "Before we continue...what's your name?"

He shrugged. "I wouldn't tell you. Call me Paul." He pointed further down the trail. "Here it is better."

We followed the trail, the crowd of men following us closely. Paul put his hand behind my neck, steering me like a domineering husband with a submissive wife. There, hanging from a tree, was a rattan chair, swinging in the breeze. It had a beat-up pillow with a fern pattern on the seat and backrest. The seat was at waist height. In the chair, a pair of older men were finishing up. The middle-aged bottom grunted in delight as the senior man plowed into him. As our entourage showed up, the senior gave a sigh of satisfaction as he burped his semen into the man's ass. When he pulled out, his long, thin cock fell with a slap to his thigh, splashing semen on the earthen floor below. He put his impressive cock in his polyester pants and helped his partner out of the chair.

Paul pushed me forward roughly. Without any hesitation, I slid into the chair, lifting my knees toward my chest. My serpentine cock hung between my legs, covering my hole. Paul stared at it and gestured for me to move it out of the way. I picked it up and lay it across my thigh, pressing until it wedged in the space between my waist and leg. Paul knelt and tongued my hole, locking his lips and forcing saliva into my anus. I squirmed and wriggled, enjoying the wet sensation and the pressure of his tongue against my ass. Paul stood and held his hard cock against my rectum.

Without asking if I was ready, he forced himself inside. I was looser this time; the pain was momentary. The crowd had formed a circle around the chair, jacking their boners. They let out a gasp as Paul rammed past my second hole in a smooth slide. I was opened up now. The hole clapped softly. Paul held the sides of the swinging chair, pushing it gently back and forth so I slid up and down his shaft with very little effort.

"You like that, bitch?"

His abusive words sent shivers of pleasure through my body. "Yes, sir."

"Good boy." He slapped my ass, and it tightened

around his shaft. I watched his biceps bulge and contract in an ever more rapid clip as he pushed and pulled me to him. Laying back in this wicker swing chair, I had no work to do at all except hold my legs and allow him in. It was sheer joy.

"Fuck him harder!" Someone in the crowd cried out.

"Shut the fuck up!" Paul's face contorted into a snarl. It turned me on more. Despite his rude retort, he did exactly as he was asked. I felt him pull me hard to his waist and push me away even harder, roughly dragging his cock through my shitter. The saliva had begun to dry out, so he stopped, snorted, and spat a thick loogey on his shaft. It was a mixture of saliva and clear mucus. I didn't have time to be disgusted because the relief was so profound. It was slick and buttery. My burning asshole accepted the salve and relaxed again.

I felt the first drops land on my cheek. Someone in the crowd had popped off again. I wiped the goo and used it to lubricate my cock head while I stroked it. Paul didn't tell me to stop like he had before. My already enormous cock engorged and lifted off my leg. I held on as it rose towards my chest. The head aligned with my mouth; I needed only to crane my neck forward in order to lick the swelling corona, so I did. I ran my tongue along the underside, reaching up and forward to lick precum from the slit. Paul concentrated on ramming my ass hard and fast. Beads of sweat dripped from his brow onto my pubic hair. He looked up and saw me licking myself.

"Save it for me." He said it gently, like a lover whispering to his mate. His kindness was somewhere between his two personalities, like a happy medium. He was dominant but not rude. The momentary affection had a physical effect. Precum started gushing from my cock. Paul pulled the head to his mouth and drained it. That set off another reaction: my gut muscles started contracting rhythmically, just as Paul's had done.

I had never felt an anal orgasm; it sent me over the moon. I was afraid I would bust a nut right there, disappointing my lover. I turned to my old saw for delaying orgasm: macaroni and cheese. I don't know why that food was an instant boner-killer, but it was. I pictured the gooey creamy pasta bubbling in an oven, and my cock softened. I couldn't come as long as I kept that strange image in my mind.

Paul surprised me when he came without warning. He grunted softly, and deposited his warm load in my gut. When he pulled out, I expelled a few drops which landed softly on the ground. The crowd had grown. When Paul stepped away, he gestured to my ass, offering up to all comers.

A tall, thin, hairless man with a large nose stepped forward. I glimpsed his short, very fat cock. The short ones tended to hurt, especially the fatties. My ass was lubed with cum, but that wouldn't be enough. I saw him produce a tube of KY Jelly and sighed with relief. He greased his cock liberally with the slippery gel and used a finger to work some inside my hole. He spread my cheeks. His cock wasn't as prone to gravity as the longer ones.

"You ready?"

I nodded eagerly.

He aimed with his hips, and entered me hands-free. It hurt, as I expected, but it didn't take long before it felt good.

Fat Cock said, "You got a lot of cum up there, don'tcha?"

I nodded.

He said, "That's how I like it. Gonna add mine to the mix."

He held my cheeks apart so his cock wouldn't fall out. It was thick and just long enough to press on my prostate. He couldn't take long strokes, but the short strokes were enough to repeatedly push the button, causing my massive cock to drool. He leaned forward and caught the clear fluid on the tip of his tongue.

Fat Cock said, "Fuck, you're big. You taste good, too."

I could swear I felt his cock grow a little longer inside me. It was my imagination, but I'm sure he got harder as he talked dirty.

"Little whore, you like it when Daddy fucks his little girl, don't you?"

I wasn't really into the role-playing, but I knew it would hurry him along to orgasm. I had never been in a group scene like this, and I realized I wanted all the cum I could get. It was early in the afternoon, but this crowd looked like it could last until long after sunset if things didn't move along. I caressed and pinched Fat Cock's smooth nipples and chest.

He threw his head back and said, "Fuck, you're gonna make me come!" And he did. It tickled my rectum. When he pulled out, I felt air blow in my hole, and his cum leaked out. He hadn't planted it as deep as Paul had. I tried to clamp down on my hole, but the fat cock had stretched my man pussy; it wouldn't stem the flow.

Next a black man with a modest cock plowed me, calling me the "n" word and slapping my ass hard. While he was working on my ass, a beefy bear of a man put his long, fat cock in my mouth and I sucked him off. His breath grew short, and he pulled out.

The bear said, "Not yet. I wanna fuck you."

After the black man, the bear slid easily inside me, pushing past that hole. He was as long as Paul, with a small head. His shaft was very thick in the middle, so each time he pushed in or pulled out, I felt my hole stretch painfully. The pain subsided as he progressed. Shallow breaths led to an intense orgasm. He shouted so loudly the others shushed him. The last thing I needed was for the cops to show up. But this was a very isolated spot. The swinging chair would have been removed if the cops or park maintenance knew it was there. I was safe in the tree room, gaping, dripping with cum, waiting for the next cock to load me up with jizz.

As men zipped up and walked away, new onlookers arrived, so the crowd never seemed to shrink. It may have gotten bigger. Cocks of every shape and size plowed my ass, packing my ass with more and more cum. Every so often, I blew a gob out. My hole was too loose to stop it. I had three or four types of lube up there: Crisco, KY, Corn Huskers, and Albolene. It was a slippery mess, but it kept my sore ass from getting raw.

By midnight, the last of the onlookers took me and filled me. I looked around for Paul, but he had driven off in his Ferrari, leaving me stranded.

When I got out of the chair, I stumbled and fell to my knees. Nobody was there to help me up. I gingerly stood, swaying. My ass was a rubbery hole, unable to hold back as gravity dumped load after load of cum on my pants, which were still around my ankles. I pulled them up, groaning. I stumbled out of the park to a bus stop. My jeans were sopping wet in the crotch and ass.

The bus took me home to my sleepy neighborhood. I rang the bell. When I stood to get off, I felt a flush of embarrassment. I had leaked a puddle of cum on the seat. I had nothing to wipe it with. I pitied the next person to sit there. If it was a woman, she'd probably have an immaculate conception!

Gingerly, I took the steps one by one and flopped down on my bed, falling into a dreamless sleep.

When my bruised and battered hole tightened up, I returned to the chair, and repeated the endless orgy. I never saw Paul again. Maybe he flew back to his palace in Saudi Arabia or his villa in Greece. I never knew his real name, but I was grateful he had shown me the path to paradise.

ABOUT THE AUTHORS

Peter Schutes is the nom de plume of a prolific and acclaimed novelist. As Peter Schutes, he is the author of Adult Erotic Fiction such as <u>The Slaves of Rome</u>, <u>Dark as a Dungeon</u>, <u>The Gospel of Priapus</u>, and <u>Panama Heat</u>. He writes in the style of vintage pulp authors from the 1960s and 1970s. He lives in Los Angeles.

Chuck Idgaf is a relatively new queer author. Deep into middle age, Chuck decided to broaden his hobbies, writing very erotic short stories. Initially, he just shared them with friends. The collaboration with Jim Dandy is the first time his work will be widely available. Chuck has a fondness for bears and daddies, so those tend to be common themes. He also likes stories about coming out, first times, and exploring new experiences. If you can't figure it out from the dialogue in his stories, Chuck grew up in the Deep South. He now lives in the Coachella Valley, California, with his husband.

J. W. Steed is pleased to be making his pseudonymous debut in this anthology. He is the author of more than a dozen mainstream novels and also writes memoir and humorous essays. He teaches creative writing in the metro NYC area and is active in the Science Fiction and Fantasy Writer's Association (SFWA).

OTHER BOOKS FROM PETER SCHUTES PUBLISHING

E-books and Paperbacks

The Able Seaman

The Anaconda Copper

The Autobiography of Peter Schutes

Backwoods Delivery

Big Bodies of All Sizes

Big Hole River

Bobbing Buoys and Salty Seamen

Bunkhouse Buddies

The Butt Baby

Chopper Jock

Cloistered

Confessions of a Rodeo Clown

Dark as a Dungeon

Demonic Deception *aka* Deceived, Cursed & Blessed

Desert Island Daddies

The Expectant Member

Firehouse Lovers

The Fish

Five Erotic Tales

The Gospel of Priapus

Hercules and Lippos

Hobo Honey

Hot Blue Collars

Hotshot

Like the Greeks Do

Logger's Delight

Muscle Bottom

Panama Heat

Satanic Seductions

Satan's Sissy Boy

The Slaves of Rome

The Thigh Baby

Under the Boardwalk

World's Biggest

***** Coming Soon *****

Hoboes, Hustlers, and Jailbirds

Small Cockpits and Big Hangars

Tales of Two Daddies

More Tales of Two Daddies